BLOOD ON THE SUN

A NOVEL BY ROGER ANDERSON
EDITED BY STEPHANIE ANDERSON

Tell your father's story!

BENGHAZI, NORTH AFRICA

JULY 28, 1943

A sleek new B-24 drones into view, circles the bulldozed strip of Libyan Desert like a swan over a glassy pond. The control tower shoots a green flare and the great bird swoops down on final approach.

Like a lover, the pilot handles the controls with smooth caresses. Red Rider knows this baby and all of her intricacies. He could handle her blindfolded. His flaming red hair is slicked back and tamed, and at 24, he is the old man on the crew of ten in this ship. Stocky and medium height, you can tell the years of farm work shaped and molded him, as the California sun blazed his skin and blotched it with freckles.

"Gear down," he tells his copilot.

"Gear down," Skeeter repeats. He is tall and thin, dark hair with a young boy face at 22, and he obediently pulls the lever. They hear the WHOOSH of air as wheels drop out of their wells and the plane trembles and shimmies through thermal currents over the hot desert. Red eases the throttles back, feels her descent.

"Half flaps.'

"Half flaps," Skeeter complies.

The great ship settles gracefully to earth with four roaring engines kicking up a massive cloud of red sand, and she rolls smoothly toward the distant hardstand area crowded with B-24's.

Inside the right waist of the ship, Arnie, a nineteen-year-old Algerian/American Jew, short and wiry with a loud Brooklyn mouth that makes up for his size, leans out the window.

"Holy shit! This looks like the surface of the moon!" His voice booms over the engines. "Hey ya's guys, we're on the moon!"

Steve, 18 and even smaller than Arnie, crawls out of the tail turret and playfully shoves Arnie out of the way. His sweet, Midwestern face cracks a huge grin.

"It's the moon alright. I'd know it anywhere."

Arnie pushes himself up next to Steve and the two squint out the window through the thick dust and blasting heat. Mike, 18 years young, leaves his radio post and squeezes between the two gawkers to catch the view.

"Looks more like the asshole of creation. Damn! What happened to the country club air bases with beautiful girls and champagne?" His pasty white, school-boy face and New Hampshire accent are a dead give-away that he's never seen land like this before.

Arnie slaps him on the back. "All a hoax, man. The wild blue yonder and all that bull. If this looks anything like your asshole, we're in trouble."

"Shut up!" Mike socks him in the gut. Then he turns and calls into the ship, "Jacob, Gus, come here and check it out."

A voice shouts back from deep inside, "Why the hell would I want to look at a stinkin' desert?"

Gus peers over the gun he's been polishing incessantly and looks out of his left waist window. His melancholy face is flushed and sweaty, yet his flight suit is zipped up tight and proper. At 18, he clings to the rules. Rules make life predictable. Though there is nothing predictable in war, if he can just keep his small space in order, he can manage. He sees the dust cloud and lifeless land flash by and he mumbles miserably to himself, "This ain't Minnesota."

The ship rolls to a stop in a vacant hardstand. Her shiny skin reflects the sun, contrasting with the dust-caked, beat-up B-24's sitting around her. Many have holes in odd places, entrance and exit wounds from shrapnel, bullets and cannon shells. Some have frayed and tattered wings. They look like plucked chickens next to Red Rider's beautiful, unscathed bird.

Arnie, Steve, Mike and Gus drop out of the bomb bay to the ground, dragging duffel bags with them. Arnie steps into the sun and immediately shrinks back under the plane, his hand over his face. "We're gonna fry out here!"

The four young men cluster together under the plane's belly like fearful chicks and squint at the sun-scorched world.

Skeeter and Red make their way toward the bomb bay, but Hal jumps in front of them, blocking the way. The nineteen-year-old, pudgy Kansas farm boy-turned-airman bubbles with eager innocence. "Everything checks out fine, Lieutenant. She made the trip humming."

"Good," Red smiles at his exuberance. "Now grab your bag and get out of here before we all cook in this metal bird."

"Yessir!" After a snappy salute, he turns and pounds down the catwalk.

Red lets his voice echo through the plane. "Dom, Tex, let's go!" Skeeter moves past him hauling his duffel. Dominick emerges from the nose, duffel in one hand, several thick books balanced in the other. He smiles his easy-going, white-tooth smile at Red. Italian-American, the twenty-year-old from Richmond, Virginia has dark hair over a handsome olive face and speaks with a soft, slow, Southern drawl.

Red nods at him. "Catch up on your reading, Dom?"

"Ralph Waldo Emerson at 25,000 feet. Doesn't get better than that. Y'all oughta try it." He hefts the books and rolls his dark eyes as if he were talking about an excellent wine.

Tex follows behind and shoves Dominick to move on. He's a weather-beaten, lanky twenty-year-old, looking like he just got off his horse, except for the open flight suit over the sweaty white T-shirt under it. He adjusts his worn black Stetson over his forehead. "Damn, if this ain't the ugliest range I seen yet. We're in hell now."

Red pushes him toward the bomb bay. "Thanks for the location, Navigator. Let's go see if the Devil's home."

The crew huddles in the safety of the plane's shade,

watching a truck speed across the desert toward them, followed by a plume of red dust. A duffel drops from the plane and Jacob hops down beside it, raising his own cloud. He's 18 and a Jew from Manhattan, but not the warm cuddly kind. His flight suit is already peeled back to let the body heat escape and he pulls a T-shirt out of the duffel, puts it on his head draped over his neck for instant shade. "Gentiles," he snorts at the others. "And here I thought you were from the country and knew how to take care of yourselves."

They all ignore the comment and Jacob's resourcefulness, as the truck skids to a dusty halt. A corporal leans out, spits a puddle of black sledge in the sand and grins with missing and stained teeth. He adjusts the wad in his lip to speak.

"Corporal Hammon, at your service."

The crew scramble onto the truck benches, and Red slides in beside Hammon, who leans uncomfortably close. He is older and scraggly, with his dishwater hair matted under his cap and the odor of sour tobacco wafts over everyone.

"Where'll it be, Lieutenant?" he asks with nauseating enthusiasm. "Take ya anywhere ya wanna go. 'Cept away. Ha!" He slaps the seat back and laughs like he's drowning.

Red tries to hold his breath. "Headquarters first, then living quarters."

"Yessir. Here we go!"

The truck whips a 360 while the crew clings wildly to their seats, and then zips across the sand. Hammon grips the steering wheel in both hands and leans forward, looking like a mad driver in a hot rod race. He manages to keep talking despite the size of the wad in his teeth.

"Must of just come from the States, right Lieutenant? That's a mighty fine bird you flew in on."

"Yep," Red replies, "We're a green crew and that's our baby."

Hammon hurls a brown stream from his mouth. The crew watches as it flies past their faces and leaves a yard-long splotch in the sand.

"Bet you picked up that pretty plane in Topeka, Kansas," he says and leans toward Red to wink.

"How'd you know that?"

Hammon grins proudly, "That's my home town. Everybody works at the factory and if I'd knowed you was comin' I'd of had you go to dinner with my folks. Ma would of made a chocolate cake for me and I'd of split it with ya. Too bad we don't get told these things ahead a time." He yanks the steering wheel to avoid a pothole, making Red grab hold tight.

"Yeah, too bad."

They approach a group of scattered buildings, some tin, some cement, all in various degrees of disrepair.

"Y'all are lucky to be here, ya know," Hammon sputters.

"Really? How's that?" Red asks, and looks to see if the corporal is being sarcastic. Nothing he can see would make him think of luck. This place looks like the landscape of some war veteran's nightmare.

"We got the best CO in the 8th Air Force," Hammon continued. "Colonel Jensen. The fly boys'd follow him anywhere. He's the best."

He skids to a halt in front of a cement block, scarred from machine gun bullets, with a hand painted sign that says: 44TH HDQTRS. Red hops out, wading through the cloud, and disappears inside. The rest of the crew sits glumly in the truck, looking around in shock, sweating in their flight suits. Even Gus quietly unzips his and peels it off of his arms. Only Jacob seems to be enjoying the shade of his T-shirt headpiece and his dark eyes seem resigned to the baked desert. Now that they are not moving, the sun sucks the juice right out of them, except for Hammon. He sits there patiently, sucking and spitting and shifting that blackened wad around in his mouth. Mike and Hal cover their noses.

Red steps into the inner office, which is a Spartan room with a desk and two chairs. He salutes. Colonel Jensen stands from behind his desk and returns the salute. At 32 he is an old man for this war and he exudes the air of a natural commander. He is average build and lean with what must be sandy hair that has been buzz cut. His face is war-hardened, but his eyes are kind and they soften his look and put Red at ease. Both men sit in the two chairs comfortably.

"Lieutenant Rider, I assume," Colonel Jensen says with a disarming smile. Red nods. "And you brought a new B-24?"

Red smiles back. "Yessir. We calibrated the instruments, did the test flights. She purrs like a kitten."

"Good," Colonel says then sighs heavily. "We have a tough mission coming up in 3 days. We need that plane. Your crew will get one of our old planes."

He raises a hand as Red starts to protest. "Think about it," he says, leaning forward, his compassionate eyes boring into Red. "If you were a crew who'd flown a bunch of missions and had a shot-up ship, don't you think you'd deserve a new plane from a green crew?"

Red groans, frustrated, but what can he say? "When you put it that way, Colonel. I guess." All he can think about is how will he tell his crew the news. He wonders which one of the hole-ridden, wing-tattered crates they will be assigned to. This desert post is getting more depressing by the minute.

Colonel Jensen's voice softens, "You'll get a veteran plane that isn't pretty, but it flies. Ground crews are installing bomb bay tanks now."

He stands up and Red takes the cue. "Get your crew settled and make yourselves useful to the ground crew in the morning. We're scheduled for a practice mission tomorrow afternoon."

Red hesitates to leave, "Bomb bay tanks? Must be a long mission." He can feel his guts tightening. Here they are and it's nothing but real war now. He and the crew will have no choice but to suck up their resentments and obey.

Colonel nods, "Fourteen hours. Yes, a long one."

"Are we bombing Tokyo?"

"Just about. The location is top secret until the night's briefing. That's how important it is to us. That's all I can tell you." Colonel shrugs and his face relaxes for a moment. "Let me know if you and your crew need anything. And Red, I'm glad you're here. I assume everyone calls you that?"

"Yessir, unavoidable."

The colonel picks a paper off of his immaculate desk and hands it to Red. "This is a pass to get into the mock up. You and your officers need to study the target model carefully. There's a lot riding on the success of this mission and you'd better be prepared."

"Yessir." Red's skin prickles with nerves. The colonel sounds dead serious and suddenly the weight of responsibility seems heavy on Red's inexperienced shoulders.

As if reading his mind, Colonel Jensen says softly, "You'll do fine." He extends his hand and they shake. Red turns to leave, thoroughly overwhelmed.

"Thank you, sir," he mumbles.

The crew notices the look on their lieutenant's face the moment he steps out of headquarters.

"Boss ain't happy, boys," Arnie says.

Skeeter studies Red as he climbs back in the truck. "Didn't go so good?" he asks tentatively.

"No." And Red doesn't offer anymore.

Corporal Hammon spits a lake of sledge and starts up the truck. "Where to?" he asks jovially as if unaware of Red's trepidations.

"Show us where we eat, shit and sleep, in that order."

With a hiccuping sputter, Hammon slaps the steering wheel. "Yessir!" He slams the truck into gear and shoots across the sand. The crew clings to whatever they can grab. They zoom by a bombed out building with a hole the size of a tank in the cement wall. Smoke rises from the corrugated tin roof.

"That's the cook shack, Lieutenant. You line up with your mess kit and they'll serve you gourmet C-rations. Make ya wish you'd brought your stomach pump." He snorts and laughs through tobacco juice.

"Right," Red says, leaning away from him.

They pass a long, tin-roof building with canvas sides. The stench wafts over them in the moving truck.

"That there's the latrine," Hammon says. "Not fancy, but if ya get dysentery, it'll be home-sweet-home." He stops the truck on a sandy rise and a tent city sprawls across the desert before them. Old crashed aircraft of every kind, probably dating back to the beginning of aviation, rise up like skeletons among the tents.

"There you go, sir. Benghazi Hilton. No reservations needed. Careful of the rooms with a view of the latrine. Smells like an Arab cemetery. Just mosey on down there and pick anything that looks unlived-in. The way this war goes, that can change on a daily basis. It's all the same where ever you pick. Desert dust'll get ya anyways."

Red gets out of the truck. The others have already jumped out as soon as it came to a stop. "Well, thanks a lot, Corporal. It's been most enlightening."

Hammon spews a great juicy stream, and his eyes twinkle merrily. "At your service, sir, anytime." With that he zooms off with the truck. The crew is left in the dust, duffel bags in hand, looking at Red like lost boys. He can feel the weight of their needs pulling on his shoulders. Skeeter asks what they have all wanted to know.

"So what happened back in Headquarters?"

Red looks at the tender faces of these would-be warriors and doesn't hesitate. "There's a big mission coming up and we don't get to keep our plane." They collectively gasp.

Hal grabs his arm, "How come, Lieutenant?"

"Yeah," says Arnie, "it's our plane!"

"I engineered that ship," Hal blurts, his face reddening more now than from the sun.

Red shakes his head, "Get used to it. We take orders and that's it. Maybe someday we'll get shot up enough to deserve a new plane. That's all there is to it." He raises his hands to ward off more protests, seeing the utter disappointment in his crews' eyes. "Come on now, let's get settled in."

He leads the boys into tent city and they wander around, looking for a vacant group.

A man is shaving, stripped to the waist, with a mirror hung from his tent pole. His skin is sun-baked brown, and though he stands in the shade of his tent, his back glistens with sweat.

"Howdy, neighbor!" Red says amicably. The man turns to them, his face half shaven, and frowns with annoyance.

"Another load of Navy rejects," he scoffs. "Welcome to Paradise."

Red grins, not put off by the man's sarcasm. "We heard you're the official receptionist. Would you kindly direct us to our quarters? Seems we're lost already."

The neighbor rolls his eyes and points with the razor. "On the other side of that wrecked German ME-109 you'll find yourselves some empties. They're all yours."

"Thanks, we'll be sure and tip you on our way back."

The neighbor returns to shaving with a grunt. "Don't mention it."

The crew walks around the skeleton of the German plane, perhaps wondering if the German pilot is buried in the sand there too, and they enter a cluster of vacated tents. The flaps hang in ghostlike silence, with not a soul around, not even a footprint. A few personal objects lie abandoned, like a boot, a half-buried towel, a candy bar wrapper. They pause for an eerie moment, wondering what happened to the previous occupants. No one wants to think about what would be left behind if they didn't come back from a mission. Again, the finality of death in this war hits them like the blast of desert heat.

"Skeeter and I'll take this one," Red says, trying to break the moment. He points to the tent closest to the wrecked plane. He walks over to the corroded frame of the wreck and puts a hand on it, dispelling the gloom. "That'll make a good clothes line."

"Or a landmark on a dark night after a few beers," Skeeter

adds.

"That too," Red agrees.

The crew drags duffel bags toward the various tents in the circle. Arnie blocks Steve from entering one. "I'm bunkin' with Gus or Hal or Mike. Hell, I'll even invite Jacob the Grouch so long as he doesn't snore like you."

Steve looks offended. "You can hear me just as good from the one next door, so relax."

Arnie turns to the others for support. "I understand you country boys got a cure for snoring. Corn cob up the ass."

Steve pushes past him and moves into the tent. "Turn around and I'll use yours, asshole."

Mike moves away from them to the opposite side of the circle. "You guys are sick."

"I'll bunk with ya, Steve. City slickers are too damn delicate," Tex says, following Steve into the tent.

Dominick nods after them, "Tex can sleep through anything. Wish I could."

Red tosses his duffel on the cot in his tent and steps back out. "Listen up, crew." All movement in and out of tents ceases. They look at him like obedient puppies. "They want me and Skeeter, Tex and Dom to go look at a mock-up of the mission's target. The rest of you can set up house nice and homey while we're gone. And don't kill each other."

Skeeter shakes his head, "They sure don't give you any time to get used to the idea, do they?"

"This is what we trained for, Boys. Time to get busy," Red says. "Drop your duffels and let's go."

The three officers follow Red back around the German plane to the neighbor's tent.

"Now what?" Neighbor asks with a frown. He is now wearing a uniform shirt, freshly shaven, but looking bored as he sits on a crate in a patch of tent shade.

Red bows before him with elaborate hand gestures. "Oh, Knowledgeable One, we seek guidance to the target model in the restricted area. Please tell us mere mortals, where do we go to find this special place?"

Neighbor sits back against his tent pole as if deciding whether or not to answer. There's a pause as he weights his choices, nonplussed by Red's antics. "Know where headquarters is?" Red nods humbly. "Green shack next to it, that's it."

"Why, thank you, sir," Red bows again. "Do you charge for this service?"

Neighbor cracks a grin for the first time. "I'm thinking about starting."

"We'd like to set up an account then." Red waves and pulls his group with him. They trudge on across the scorching sand. Red taps a finger on Tex's Stetson that shades his face nicely. "Damn, Tex, I'm going to need one of those."

Tex grunts at him, "You're head's on fire anyway, boss."

"Yeah, I bet the sun can't even burn through that red hair of yours," Dominick adds.

Skeeter has unbuttoned his shirt and pulls it up over his head. "Hell, I can feel it burning through mine. Remind me not to venture out during the day."

After sweating profusely as they walk along the truck's tracks in the sand, they come to the green shack and step gratefully inside. Red hands his pass to a sergeant with fish-bowl glasses perched on his long nose, and the man leads them into the mock-up room. The small cement block room has a large table in the center and nothing else. A cardboard model of buildings, railroad tracks, haystacks, towers and a forest of smoke stacks are built on top of the table.

"Somebody's pretty artistic around here. Look at that, even has guns," Red comments. The others are silent, walking slowly around the table, grasping quickly that these buildings are something hugely important, like a factory or refinery, and noting the amazing array of guns and cannon pointing in all directions from rooftops, water towers, everywhere. The model suddenly loses its charm. Sergeant stands at attention, gazing at them with magnified eyeballs.

"As you'll learn in the final briefing," he says. "You will

pass three Initial Points before the bomb run. At the last IP, you'll fly along these railroad tracks, west to east." He produces a pointer and sweeps it over the tracks. "Your group will follow Colonel Jensen to this target – White five. You will be the last plane on the right formation and approach at zero altitude."

The group stares from him to the model and back in deadly silence. They can all see clearly that they are expected to fly into a gauntlet of firepower. Everything the enemy has will be pointed straight at them.

Sergeant continues as if he were chatting about a drive through the country. "There'll be barrage balloons over the target. You need to avoid them."

"How tall are those smoke stacks?" Red asks.

"A hundred feet."

"You mean to say, we fly along these tracks at 10 feet, fully loaded, and have to climb a hundred feet over the stacks or skirt around them, while all those guns are lighting into us," Red's voice cracks. "Is that right?"

Sergeant hesitates. Their eyes bore into him and his composure slips. He starts to speak, but stops himself and blinks at them from behind those huge lenses. Then he straightens his shoulders and clears his throat. "Yes, well, this is the most heavily fortified target in Europe. I really can't tell you anymore until the briefing. I'll leave you a few minutes to study the model." He puts down the pointer and makes a quick escape.

The four men gaze at the toy guns and cannon bristling from every point on the table. Skeeter finally voices what they are all thinking.

"And this is our first mission."

Red slaps his back, hoping to dispel the gloom. "Did you expect to live forever?"

Skeeter turns frightened eyes on him. "I'd like to live a little longer than this."

Dominick waves his hand over the model, "How are we going to dodge all that to drop the bombs?"

Tex shakes his head, "Hell, at that altitude, we are the

bomb." Skeeter and Dominick blanch, looking from Tex to the target.

Red corrals them toward the door. "I've seen enough. Let's go. And I don't want a word of this to leak to the crew. No sense in worrying them about it. They'll know soon enough.

"Wish I hadn't see that," Tex drawls. "Going to be hard to sleep now."

"I doubt that," Dominick elbows him. "You're the sleepingest guy I've ever met."

Skeeter says softly, his voice haunted, "None of us are going to be sleeping much anymore."

Red stops them at the door. He frowns at them, needing them to see his frustration. "Now all of you wipe that look off your faces. You have to act like everything is fine. This is just a routine mission, one of many to come. The rest of the crew depends on your attitude about it, so lighten up. Come on, no more worrying. We'll figure out a way to do our job and come back alive. I promise."

They watch Red's face for a moment, see the confident leader they have come to trust, and leave the building with resolute sighs.

Evening descends, mercifully calming the sun's power over the desert. Hal and Mike string a clothesline from various parts of the German craft. Steve sweeps a kind of sand lawn in front of his tent. Arnie sits on his duffel like a lounge chair, T-shirt over head and neck, Jacob-style.

The four officers step into the little enclave of tents and the crew scrambles together. Jacob and Gus quietly join them.

"Did you see it?" asks Arnie.

"Yeah, they won't tell us where it is," Red answers. "Just that it's a long flight." The other officers turn away quickly, busying themselves in their tents. Jacob stops Red with a hand to his chest.

"What does it look like?"

Red locks eyes with him, showing no hesitation. "A factory of some kind. They're not telling us until the briefing." Jacob holds his eyes a second longer, then nods and moves away. Red surveys the campsite, changing the subject. "You guys are making this real comfortable. Good job."

Mike smiles at him, "Like we've lived here ten years."

Arnie settles back on his duffel lounge. "And whenever you want to take a leak, just take him out and let it fly. Love that sand."

Hal pulls a mess kit out of his duffel and looks beseechingly at Red. "I saw other guys heading to chow. I'm hungry. Can we go yet?"

Arnie scoffs at him, "It's C-rations, for shit sake. What's the hurry?"

Hal ignores him and looks around for support. His pudgy face is twisting with serious anxiety. "But we haven't eaten anything since K-rations over Algeria."

Arnie points at his own rear end. "Take a bite outa my ass. It's a peach."

Hal turns on Arnie, hands on his hips and angry. "I'd rather starve. It looks too much like your face!"

"Enough!" Red shouts, waving his arms. "Wouldn't want Hal to starve. Get your mess kits and let's be adventurous."

Mike steps close to Hal as if to defend him and points a menacing finger at Arnie. "So back off, comedian."

Arnie twiddles an imaginary cigar. "No, you got the profession all wrong. After the war, I'm going to own the fanciest whorehouse in Brooklyn."

Mike turns away, "It'll flop. You'll eat up all the profits."

"What's the matter with that? You a vegetarian or something?"

They gather in a pack and move out. Tex gently pulls Gus from the fringes into the group. Gus walks beside Tex obediently, appreciating being included. Steve gazes at the crushed cockpit as they pass the German wreck.

"Wonder where the pilot is," he says.

"You're walking on him," Arnie snickers.

"Yeah," Steve points, "thought I saw an eyeball peeking out of the sand back there."

Mike stomps the ground, "Knock it off, you guys! That's disgusting!"

Steve leans up next to him, "Nervous, Mike?"

Hal steps between them, using his size to overshadow Steve. "Leave him alone."

Steve pokes at Hal's gut with a nonchalant grin. "Maybe you'll lose some of that fat on C-rations, eh?"

Red calls from the front of the group. "Tex, get the horse whip out in case these boys don't shut up. We're coming up on civilization here."

"Roger, Lieutenant," Tex replies.

Sun sinks into the desert and its broken rays no longer bake. The sand instantly cools.

Airmen stand in a long line, mess kits in hand, as cooks serve from the gaping hole in the wall of the cook hut. Red leads his flock toward the end of the line. A hand reaches out to him and Denny Wilson grabs him in a bear hug, smiling broadly.

"Crazy Red!" he laughs. "Fancy meeting you in this hell hole! Thought they'd send you someplace special after flight school." He is a big Californian pilot, 29, jovial and well liked by all his fly mates. Red pounds him on the back. The two crews spot each other and mingle, happy to be among familiar faces.

Red says, "They told me you all needed a shot in the arm, so here's the doctor. That's why they sent me." He touches the bars on Denny's collar. "Look at that, they made you a captain."

Denny shrugs, "They got to do something with us older guys. Make us captain to feel better about risking our lives."

"How're Janet and your kids?"

"Great," Denny's big face instantly glows. "Dan just started kindergarten and Stephanie turned three. Wait 'till I write and tell Janet you're here!"

They move up to where cooks slop unidentifiable blobs in their mess kits. Red stares at his slop.

"Don't look too close," Denny warns.

"Is this C-rations?"

"Don't smell it either," Denny directs them over to some ammunition crates doubling for benches, and they sit. Denny gives his rations a little stir, avoiding the steam, and starts eating with gusto. "In a few days you'll forget that it tastes like dog food and probably is. The stuff keeps you alive."

Red wrinkles his nose and bravely proceeds to eat. Hal seems to be the only one enjoying it. He and Mike sit off by themselves shoveling it in fast enough to go for seconds.

Denny is soon finished and he regards Red, "When did you get here?"

"Couple of hours ago. Long enough to lose our plane and hear about the mission from hell."

Denny's face darkens. "This one sounds rough."

"Aren't they all?"

Denny puts his mess kit down and looks serious. "Some are worse than others. What's your position?"

"Tail-end-Charlie right. That's all they'll tell me."

"We're tail-end-Charlie left. I'll be waving at you." Denny says it lightly, but the cheer doesn't reach his face. Red feels the need to avoid the subject and he nudges his friend.

"Looks like Gus found his old friend."

Jimmy, a young gunner from Denny's crew, in a neat and proper uniform, sits next to Gus and the two lean close to each other in quiet and private conversation.

"Thank God," Denny says. "I was worried about Jimmy finding someone to talk to. Nice, polite boys don't do too well around here."

Hal jumps up and hurries back to the chow line. Arnie yells after him, "You're not comin' near my tent if you eat any more of this crap! You'll be fartin' up a storm!"

Red shrugs apologetically to Denny.

2

Red and his crew come to a dead halt, staring into hard stand 23. The B-24 looks like it has a bad case of plane acne. Her skin is covered with welded patches and dents, long scrapes and scars.

Bob Garnes steps from beneath her, a stocky 40-year-old with powerful hairy arms and a face as scarred as the plane. Looks like he left many a bar with a few bodies lying around. He smiles, missing a front tooth, and wipes a hand to proffer.

"You must be the new crew. I'm Bob Garnes, chief mechanic." He turns and affectionately strokes the plane's nose. "And this is Betsy, finest ship on the force."

He notices the doubtful looks, the coughs from the crew, and wages a thick greasy finger at them. "Ol' Betsy will get you there and back better than those new planes. She don't look like much, but she's tough."

Red smiles, unconvinced. "We'll be depending on that. Ground crew is the most important part of a mission and I heard yours is the best. We're here to work for you this morning."

Bob's grin widens like a friendly gargoyle. He slaps Red on the back with a hard paw. "I like you guys already." He bends over and calls under the ship. "Whitie, Lowel, get out here and meet the new fellas."

The two mechanics emerge from the ship's bowels in greasy coveralls. Lowell, a lanky black boy with an amiable smile, moves up behind Bob and nods shyly at the crew. Whitie is shockingly albino, the stark whiteness of his skin in contrast to the grime smeared all over him. Even his hair is colorless, his eyes a pinky-grey. He holds his hand out to Arnie who shakes it. The others laugh at the expression on Arnie's face as he pulls his hand back covered with black grease. He laughs and wipes his hand on Whitie's suit.

"I suppose you're Lowel's brother," Arnie says.

Whitie grins, and slaps an arm around his shy partner's shoulders. "Absolutely." He gives the boy an affectionate squeeze. "Only God forgot to color me."

Bob waves his arms to stop the laughter. "First things first. Every man needs to check his station, gun and instruments. Let us know if you find anything wrong. Our biggest problem is the sand around here. Gets into everything. You gunners are going to need a lot of grease and rags."

"Go to it, boys," Red orders. The crew scrambles into the plane from the bomb bay's open belly. Red turns to Bob. "Let's hope this is the beginning of a long working relationship."

Bob regards him seriously. How many crews has he started out with who are gone forever now? He steps away, unwilling to think about it. "I'll pray for that."

Red moves slowly along the catwalk inside the plane, watching the boys check out their stations. It always amazes him to see how these awkward boys turn into cool, trained professionals once they are on the job behind their instruments. He smiles to himself, having faith in each and every one of them. Steve gives him the thumbs-up from the tail turret where his small body crams in beside the 50-caliber machine guns. He checks the swivel of his chair, the intercom and the oxygen.

On the flight deck, Red sits beside Skeeter and faces the great array of instruments and controls. Hal moves around them, checks switches, and reads calibers.

"Ok, Hal, start the putt-putt," Red says. "Let's see what this baby's got."

Hal nods, "Roger." He starts the generator and the plane hums with power.

"I like her purr," Skeeter comments.

The three of them listen to the mighty machine when a sudden explosion rocks them from outside the plane. They all jump to their feet and rush out at once.

Outside, the crew stops short at the edge of their hardstand area as medics hurry into the neighboring B-24. The crew looks up at the top turret and sees blood splattered over the window. After a moment they pull the unconscious gunner out, as blood gushes from his mangled hand and forearm. They wrap it up as they lay him on the stretcher then pick it up and trot off to the field hospital.

Hal runs a shaky hand through his hair. "He must have touched off the firing pin."

"His career's over, just like that," says Mike.

Skeeter looks thoughtfully after the disappearing medics and says softly, "Who's to say he didn't just save his life. No more missions for him."

Red gently pushes his men back to the plane. The neighboring crew stands there in shock. They'll have a clean up job to do now. Red's crew silently crawls back inside, each to his own station.

The crews of all the B-24's mill about the briefing hut, chatting and fanning themselves in the heat of day under a tin roof. The sun shines through the bullet holes in the walls, which are crudely painted with French, German and English graffiti. The words are a testimony of the many powers in control of this place. Someone painted SCREW HITLER over a black swastika.

Colonel Jensen steps into the steamy room and calls the chaos to order. "Sit down everyone. Let's get started."

Red sits next to Denny. Jimmy and Gus sit quietly together way from the noise of the others. Colonel Jensen stands on the little stage, pointer in hand, a drawing of the practice mission tacked on the wall.

"How well you do on this run will have a big impact on the mission, so pay attention," he begins. "We take off at 2-minute intervals, starting at 1400 hours, and make formation. We fly low altitude for 40 minutes, then head for IP here." He points to the spot on the drawing. "Major Dorsey will lead 21 ships north to the Blue target, while we start our bomb run to White Five. Every ship will have 100 pound dummy bombs and I'll be watching from the lead tail turret."

He puts the pointer down, gazing over the crews, his face stern and hard, but his eyes are warm with affection for all of these men.

"Do your damnedest, boys. And good luck."

With that he hops off the stage and exits, and the crews jump up to banter with each other as they leave.

Whitie is perched on the wing and tops off the gas from the tanker truck as Red's crew approaches. "Hey, Lieutenant," he calls to them. "I just pissed in the tank – 100 proof! You'll take off like a rocket." His laughter almost knocks him off the wing.

"Let it be noted in case we crash or blow up," Red says solemnly. "Whitie pissed in the gas."

Arnie yells at him, "Yo, Whitie, why don't you bottle it and sell it as a secret weapon."

Whitie grins down at them. "Good idea! You wanna be my business manager?"

"Hell no!" Arnie waves dismissively.

The crew enters the plane and finds Bob and Lowel checking gauges. "Is she ready to fly?" Red asks.

"Like a striped-ass ape," Bob assures him proudly.

"I'd rather she flew like an airplane. I'm not checked out on striped-ass apes." Red slaps him on the back and heads for the nose.

Tex is at his tiny desk and he studies the desert map, calculating navigation. Dominick is tucked all the way into the nose beside his guns, surrounded by window, a bird's eye view of the world and one of the most vulnerable spots on the plane.

Red peers into Dominick's space, "Always thought you had the best seat in the house, Dom."

"I'm beginning to wonder about my line of work. Just scraped old blood off the gun. That couldn't be good."

"No worries," Red says with confidence he is now good at

faking. "You're riding with me."

Dominick glances up at him and meets his eyes. The uncertainty there is real, but commitment to the job overrides all feelings. "I'll hold you to that, boss."

Tex pushes the Stetson back from his forehead and looks at his watch. "Comin' up on 1400 hours. Let's give this baby a whirl."

Outside a flare shoots from the control tower and explodes in a shower of green. Bob has hurried to his position, standing beside number two engine with a fire extinguisher in hand. "Let her rip!"

"Clear!" Red calls out his window.

"Clear!" Bob calls back.

"Energize two," Red tells Skeeter, who flips the switch and they hear number two catch, cough, and whine. "Energize 1,3, and 4." They listen to the power grow until the whole ship buzzes like a monster held in check. Giving the thumbs-up out of his window, Red releases Betsy to roll into the long line of 37 planes waiting to take off. The whole crew watches from their various windows as each plane takes off, and the line advances twenty feet every two minutes.

"Gonna take an hour to get off at this rate, " Skeeter comments.

Dominick's voice reaches them through the intercom. "I'm dying of lung cancer with all this dust!"

Tex calls on the intercom, "Incentive to be a lead crew."

Colonel Jensen, squeezed tightly into the tail turret of the lead plane, watches the migrating-geese formation and signals his pilot to slowly drop to the "deck" at 10 feet above the desert floor. The huge Flying Liberators roar over the land at 200 miles an hour.

Betsy is last on the right formation. Red holds her there, but gets antsy for some fun. "Let's play with her a little," he suggests as he flattens her belly to the ground, bobbing up over boulders and brush, her great wings tipping side to side. The steering vibrates in his hands as he holds her steady and objects flash by far too quickly.

The intercom crackles. "Yeeeehhhhaaawww!" Tex shouts. "Ride her cowboy!"

Dominick yells, "That rock came too close. Watch it, boss!"

Steve's voice comes from the tail, "Yeah! You just scraped my ass off!"

Mike interrupts from the radio station, "Lieutenant, they're calling us, wanting to know what we're doing down here."

"Practicing evasive action," Red smiles. "You tell them." He may hear complaints later back at the base, but for now he can't resist the feel of that powerful and heavy bird made light by her surging engines, tearing up the desert floor. It he doesn't make it through this war, he thinks to himself, as least he will have lived and been thrilled.

The lead ship turns off the IP and opens bomb bay doors. A patch of white chalk lines flashes beneath them and the lead drops it's bombs. All other ships drop theirs.

Tex says into the intercom, "That didn't look like much."

"The real thing will look like a target, I guarantee," Red replies.

Back in the briefing hut, Colonel Jensen paces on the stage, his hands clasped behind his back and a hint of a smile on his proud-father face. "You boys did good," he begins as everyone finally settles down. "Looks like we clobbered the target." They all cheer and pat each other on the back. "Formation was a little sloppy, especially with tail-end-Charlie right hedgehopping." He looks meaningfully at Red's group.

"Now you know why they call him Crazy Red," Skeeter says as others laugh.

"I just didn't want to go on oxygen like the fellas at ten feet," Red defends himself with a grin. "Besides, I like hedgehopping. It's like sex. After a while you start to enjoy it."

Colonel Jensen shakes his head, hiding a smile through the crews' laughter. "Get out of here, all of you. And in the morning, make sure your planes are ready for the mission." He leads the young, playful men out of the briefing hut, glad for their moment to banter. There will be far too few such moments to come. If they knew what awaited them, no one would laugh at all.

The morning sun, though barely up over the rim of the desert, is already blindingly brilliant. Bob leans into engine number two, perched on the top rung of a ladder. He pulls himself out and watches as Red and crew approach the hardstand.

"Good morning, Lieutenant Crazy Red," he says. "Dream about hedgehopping last night? I hear you like it better than sex."

Red looks shocked, his mouth gaping, as the crew chuckles. "Where the hell did you hear that?"

Bob puffs out his broad chest. "We're all eyes and ears on this base."

Red grabs the ladder he stands on and shakes it hard. Bob clings to the engine. "Earthquake! That'll teach you not to spread gossip." He walks over to Betsy's nose and strokes it. "I got to tell you. She looks like a madam in a two-dollar whorehouse, but she can fly."

Whitie and Lowel step out from under the plane. Whitie hooks his thumbs in his coverall pockets and swaggers proudly. "That's 'cause you got the best ground crew in the 8th Air Force."

"At least the most colorful," Red shoots back. He waves a hand at his crew. "Last check through, boys. Make it perfect."

They scramble into the plane. Lowel sidles up to Red. His voice is soft and quiet with a tinge of the South. "I fixed the temperature gauge for number three cylinder head. Was marking low. Now it's true."

Red grabs his shoulders, pats him until Lowel smiles. "Thank you, man. I couldn't ask for a better ground man."

Lowel beams a white smile across his dark face and slips

away to join Whitie.

Bob climbs down the ladder as an Arab appears, sitting on a wobbly little donkey, with his feet skimming the ground. Covered from head to toe in layers of bleached cloth, only part of his face shows. He seems out of place surrounded by modern planes and unconscious of the bustling activity from the hardstands around him. He reaches a hand from his voluminous sleeves and makes a give-me motion at Red and Bob.

"Baksheesh?" his high-pitched voice wines. "Baksheesh!"

Bob stomps a few feet closer to him and shakes his fist, "No baksheesh! Go away!" But the Arab seems unmoved. He gazes over the plane then slowly slaps his donkey and the tired little animal trudges away.

Red stares after him, "What did he mean, Baksheesh?"

Bob spits, disgusted. "Means 'free', cigarettes, candy, anything they can get off you. They just keep asking for stuff. They're a pain in the ass."

"How come they can wander around the base like that?"

"It's their stinkin' country. Ain't no fence around this place." Bob spits again, his opinion of Arabs obvious. "Some of us think they're spies left by the Germans. I don't like the way he was looking at the plane. Wouldn't be surprised if we lost crews 'cause of them. You notice the colonel doesn't tell you about the mission until you're going?" He grunts to emphasis his point, and then he climbs the ladder and sticks his head inside the engine. His voice echoes from inside: "And stay away from Arab women. Couple of weeks ago, one of our airmen lifted a woman's veil and he was found days later all cut up with his balls chopped off. Vicious killers they are, the lot of 'em."

"I'll remember that," Red says as he climbs into the plane.

On the flight deck, Whitie, Lowel and Hal are conducting a powwow over the instruments. Skeeter checks gauges and nods with satisfaction as Red enters.

"She's in good shape. Everything checks out."

Red nods, thinking. He flips the intercom switch on. "Anyone want to go swimming in the Mediterranean this afternoon?"

A chorus of responses floods over the system. The boys on the flight deck look eager and willing. Hal is the only one who seems worried. "I never swam in an ocean before."

Lowel looks surprised. "Where you from?"

"Kansas."

Whitie bows his head uncomfortably. "I've been here for months now and never gone."

"His skin can't take the sun," Lowel explains sadly.

Red pipes up, "You can tell us how to get there, can't you?"

"Sure," Whitie brightens. "There's a shuttle that runs out there from headquarters, about every hour, I expect. Be careful with the sun though. Gives me chills just thinking about it."

Red pats his back. "We'll handle it. I just want to wash off some of this damn sand."

"Yeah, boss," says Skeeter. "Your hair's fading."

Corporal Hammon's truck skids to a halt and the crew jumps out the instant it stops sliding. They dash toward the water, stripping clothes off as they run. Hammon, with his lip bulging full of tobacco, calls after Red. "Be smart and cover them bare butts in the sun."

Red waves and trots after the others. He pauses at the edge of the water, kicks off his shoes and pants, and gazes over the most pristine beach he has ever seen, even as a California boy. Gentle blue transparent waves lap over pure white sand and not a soul around. Down the beach, some wrecked landing craft rock gently in the surf. Off shore, the hull of a ship rests, and Red feels the presence of dead soldiers on the soft breeze. How can such a beautiful spot on earth be the site of so much destruction?

"Hey, Red!" Dominick calls from the water. "Come on in, it's great!" He falls backward into the waves. The others swim and splash like seals in the water. Red finishes disrobing and wades into the bath-tepid water. Tex floats on his back, his Stetson still shading his head. Gus sits in shallow water in his underwear and T-shirt.

"You ok, Gus?" Red asks on his way in. Gus squints up at him meekly.

"Yessir. Just relaxing here. Don't want to get too burned."

Red tousles the hair on the boy's head before sinking into the deeper water. Jacob swims by, demonstrating a racer's crawl in fine form. Hal and Mike bob like corks and laugh gleefully.

"I never knew water could feel like this!" Hal exclaims. "Wait 'til I write home about it."

"Never felt anything so warm," Mike agrees. "No more summers on Cape Cod for me. I'm going tropical from now on."

Steve stands in knee-deep water and lets the sun bake him dry. Arnie dog-paddles by, "Hey Steve, what's that hanging off your dick?"

Steve glances down at his anatomy. "A piece of skin. What does it look like?"

Arnie jumps up and starts to wave at the others. "You guys! Come here and look at Steve's dick!" They swim over and surround him.

"I never seen skin hanging off a dick before," Hal says in awe.

Steve, unruffled, turns slowly for all to see. "The doctor who circumcised me was drunk. I guess he passed out before he finished."

"Good thing he didn't cut it all off," Mike breathes.

Arnie points a disdainful finger, "Doesn't it bother your girl when you're having sex?"

"Naw," Steve says with pride, "She's too impressed with how good I am." Arnie snickers and swims away a few feet.

Jacob stops his laps back and forth, looks scornfully at Steve's genitalia and says, "Why don't you get the damn thing cut off?"

Steve grabs a hold of the flap of skin. "It makes a great handle." He demonstrates by holding it up and pissing at his audience. They fall back, screaming.

"You should hire him after the war to do a freak show in your whorehouse," Mike says to Arnie.

"No, my place is going to be a class act."

Red floats luxuriously nearby. "What are you going to do after the war, Mike?"

Mike looks offended. "You mean you can't tell? Radio broadcaster, of course."

"Who'll hire you with that New England accent of yours?"

"New Hampshire radio, of course. We take care of our own."

Skeeter paddles into the cluster. "I'm going to marry Suzie first thing when I get back. Then I'm going to copilot on commercial airlines. Dad says that pays good."

"You won't catch me dead on one of those commercial, elevator-style flights," Red says emphatically. "No sir, not me. Boring, no offense to you, Skeeter. It's just that I'm going to Hollywood and if nothing else, I'll fly stunts for movies."

"I'm taking over the farm," Hal says with assurance. "My dad's been growing corn for years, but you know, the future's in soy. Soon as it's mine, it'll be soy all the way."

Red splashes at Dominick, "Dom's going to be an English professor. I can see it now. Stacks of books on his desk, spouting poetry 'til people think he's crazy."

Dominick shines one of his sun-rise smiles. "Yeah, maybe."

Corporal Hammon slams on the brakes next to Headquarters and the crew jumps out. They head out on the path to the tents, still playful and happy from their afternoon swim. Red gets out and moves around the truck to Hammon's side to shake his hand. "Thanks for the ride. Seems like it did some good for the boys."

Hammon spits his loaded mouth and nods, "You'd think others'd figure it out and wanna spend some ocean time too, but nope. You're the smart ones."

The Headquarters door opens and Colonel Bull Madigan,

in his late 30's, steps out followed by the Commanding General, who is an older man with well-decorated lapel and a stern, quick step. The General moves briskly past with the briefest nod as Red and the Corporal salute. Bull follows him, looking like a prizefighter, hard body and a mean face.

Hammon grabs Red and pulls him close, his stinking breath overwhelming. "That's the big-wig general they flew in today. I tell ya, this mission is really big," he whispers, rolling his eyes dramatically. "The other guy is Bull Madigan. Commands the 96th. Stay out of his way. Nasty son-of-a-bitch. They say he's brutal in battle and the Luftwaffe's afraid of him. Ha! Imagine that!"

The two men have moved off a short distance to stand in the shade of a large truck, locked in conversation and disregarding their audience. Bull spits his words at the General with his fists balled tight.

"I'm telling you, we all have to throttle back to make it that far and have enough juice to pour over the target." He looks like he is squaring off and ready to raise his fists.

The General doesn't seem intimidated, but points his finger at Bull's hard chest. "Damn it, Madigan. Take orders for once in your life. We've decided the speed and altitude and that's final. Groups have to stay together. That is priority over whatever your opinion is. Enough!"

General marches over to Hammon's truck. "Corporal, you'll take us to the hardstands now."

"Yessir," Hammon sputters, after a knowing glance at Red. Bull storms after the General and sits inside, his eyes narrowed on Red, menacing. Probably wondering what he heard.

Red turns away quickly and hurries after his crew.

A carpet of crystal clear stars lies over their heads, dimmed only by the glow of the tiny fire dancing in the tent common. Music floats over the stillness from somewhere else, a 78 RPM record of a woman singing: "There'll be blue birds over the white cliffs of Dover, tomorrow when the world is free..."

Red stirs the flames to new life. Skeeter huddles close, with his long arms wrapped around his knees. Dominick sits across from them, writing in a journal, brow furrowed thoughtfully. Voices rise from a near-by tent.

"Get your fartin' ass out of here," Arnie demands.

"Shut up or I'll sit on you," Hal responds in the most threatening voice he can muster.

"Stop it, you guys," Mike says.

From another tent, the rattling sound of snoring is shockingly loud. Skeeter, staring at the fire, comments, "Listen to Tex sleep. He's amazing. Wait 'til Steve joins the snoring."

"Time for all of us to get some sleep," Red suggests.

Skeeter doesn't move, spellbound by the flames. "We're facing hell fire tomorrow and you want me to sleep?" He buries his chin in his knees and looks like a frightened kid hiding in a closet.

Dominick puts the pen down and gazes into the fire. "Wrote about the Mediterranean. If I don't make it back, I want my family to know what I've seen."

Skeeter stands suddenly and slinks off to the tent. Red and Dominick watch the fire die, the cool night silent now.

"Red, You think we'll get shot down?"

Red takes a deep breath and steadies his voice. "I got a strong feeling about tomorrow. It'll be rough, but we'll get through it."

Dominick gives him an ironic smile, "You guarantee that?"

"Stake my life on it."

"Thanks, boss. Good night then," he says, packing up his writing and heading into the tent. Red stays there and closes his eyes to hear the quiet, between the snores, and feel one of the last peaceful moments of his life.

Alone, with no one to depend on him, he can let the fear wash over him, feel it shiver up and down his spine. He hasn't been a praying man, but finds himself tilting his head back and speaking earnestly to the Creator of that magnificent sky, hoping beyond hope that he will live to see it again.

3

SUNDAY, AUGUST FIRST, 1943, 2 AM

Hundreds of flashlights bob along the desert as crews stream in to the search-light-lit cook hut. Cooks slop powdered eggs, bacon, and bread into Red and the crew's mess kits with a cup of black coffee. They move to where Denny sits on the crates with his men. Gus stands in the shadows, his hands jammed in his pockets, looking forlorn.

Red sits next to Denny. "I don't see Jimmy."

"He's grounded," Denny replies. "In the infirmary and we had to practically tie him down there. He got a cold and busted his ear drum when we flew to Algiers to pick up the General."

"Lucky to miss this mission."

"Don't tell him that," Denny says quietly. "He's furious right now, thinks he let us down." They dutifully eat the slop in their kits, but after a moment Denny turns to Red anxiously. "I'm going to ask you for a promise that I don't want you to make unless you're sincere." His eyes continue to bore into Red who gives him his full attention.

"Promise me that if this mission goes bad, you'll look out for Janet and the kids."

Red feels his stomach flop. He tries to preserve a calm, reassuring face, though his food threatens to rise back up. "Nothing's going to happen to you, Denny. I got a strong-"

Denny grabs his arm, silences him with large, haunted eyes. "Promise."

Red nods, feeling the man's grip dig in. "If anything goes wrong, I'll watch over them. You have my word."

Denny releases him and turns back to his mess kit, sighing the air out of his chest. Red takes a deep breath too, hiding the flush of anxiety he feels.

He looks around and sees that Gus hasn't eaten yet.

"You got to try and eat, Gus."

The boy steps obediently to his abandoned mess kit, takes a few bites with trembling hands. He backs away and vomits. Tex hands him an old faded bandanna to wipe his mouth, and pats him on the back.

Crews sit in raw-nerve, jittery silence as Colonel Jensen, Colonel Bull Madigan and the General take the stage. General immediately begins to pace, wound up like a grenade about to go off. Behind him, a huge map of Europe and North Africa stretches wall to wall. Yarn has been strung from a point on the Libyan Desert, all the way up to a point deep in Romania.

General stops suddenly and gazes out over the subdued crews. "Let me tell you, the greatest thrill of my life will be watching the most magnificent bomber force fly out of here today. You will strike terror in the hearts of the Germans." He begins to pace again, gesticulating with staccato hands. "You'll be flying the most important mission so far in this war – to destroy the Ploesti refineries and deprive the German war machine a third of its oil. This will shorten the war by six months and save millions of lives."

He stops and stares at the men, his face a hard chiseled mask. "Understand that if every plane is lost today, the sacrifice will be worth the outcome."

He backs up and Colonel Jensen steps forward. The silence seems weighted, lying heavily over the men who barely breathe through clenched guts.

"Your planes are carrying 1,000 pound bombs with delay-action fuses from 45 seconds to 1 hour, depending on your position in formation," the Colonel stands before them speaking in a measured tone, no dramatics. He has to focus totally on the dissemination of information, and not on the faces that he may never see again.

"Three thousand gallons of fuel at the established pace

should get you there and back." He glances at Madigan for a stern half second. "After we hit the target, your goal is to get back to Benghazi, but if you can't, try to ditch in Turkey and get back to Allied lines, or to British Malta, or Cyprus."

Colonel pauses, looks over his flock and his eyes soften with a hint of the shepherd's weighty responsibility. He says quietly, "I'm not going to stand here and tell you it'll be an easy run. B-24 is the only plane with range enough to pull this off and you men are the best, most skilled fliers out there. The time for preparation is over. The world will be a better, saver place for what you do today. Know that you have my utmost respect. Good luck."

The two Colonels and the General walk off the stage while the Chaplain steps up. He is a young and serious-face clergy dressed in a black suit with the signatory collar and he carries a large tin box that he sets on stage in front of him. Closing his eyes and bowing his head, he offers a fervent prayer to God for the success of this mission and the safety of the men. And then he stretches his hands out over the congregation and adds, "Dear Lord, if it be Thy will to take some of these good souls back to You this day. Give them peace in the knowledge that no sacrifice goes unrewarded. Give them strength to face their trial, Lord. This we ask humbly in the name of Jesus, our Savior, amen."

He stands there, hands now folded before him, and waits as the men line up and file by his box, dropping billfolds, letters, journals into it. Some men lean closer, whisper to him and the Chaplain responds with a blessing and a touch on the forehead. Dominick places his journal in the box then genuflects as Chaplain blesses him and he walks on, touching his cross to his lips.

Red follows Denny in the line. Denny opens his wallet to a picture of Janet, Dan and Stephanie. He kisses it, closing his eyes.

"Don't forget the promise," he murmurs to Red, who grips his shoulder.

It is still dark as the crew gathers at the hardstand and Skeeter hands an escape kit to each man. Mike picks up his "flimsy" radio and ducks inside the plane. Red opens his kit and sees a booklet of phrases in different languages, cash from different countries, maps, and an ancient-looking chocolate bar. Gus takes his kit, stares at it and looks sick. Red slips next to him and nudges his arm.

"You ready for this?"

Gus gazes at him, his eyes huge in his pale face. "As ready as I'll ever be, I guess."

"We'll get through this, you'll see."

The boy nods, head bowed, and follows the others into the plane.

Inside the flight deck, Red, Skeeter and Hal run through the final equipment checks. Red leans out the window. The ground crew is outside walking around, checking everything with flashlights.

"How she look?" Red calls.

"Set to go," Bob says.

"You tell Whitie, he better not have pissed the gas this time."

Whitie ducks under the wing, grins up at Red. "Lowel and I both pissed. Now you're really blessed."

Lowel's voice reaches them from the shadows. "You just come on back from this, Lieutenant."

Red lifts his chin to Bob. "Aren't you guys going to wish us luck?'

"You kidding?" Bob grabs the plane in a wide hug. "I want my Betsy back. I'll be sweatin' it for the next 14 hours. Good luck! And give 'em hell!"

Red shuts the window with a thumbs-up. Now it begins.

Betsy taxis to last position for take off as ships roar down the runway and peel off at the last second to circle above and wait. Predawn light barely glows and casts strange shadows as the great birds hover above the growing dust cloud.

"Can you feel the weight of her?" Red asks and Skeeter glances nervously at him.

"We've never taken off with so much before."

"Piece of cake," Red assures, hiding his doubts.

Betsy is finally next in line. The plane ahead of her takes off down the runway. It starts to tip up for the sky when an engine blows out and it dives off the runway, plows into the ground in a huge explosion.

Skeeter gasps and freezes.

"Twenty degrees flaps," Red orders.

"You're not going-"

"You heard me."

Skeeter snaps to it. "Roger," and he does as bid.

Red pushes to full throttles and the ship trembles and charges forward like a thoroughbred out of the chute.

"We're not going to make it by them," Skeeter says in a strangled whisper as the crashed ship's flames shoot back toward them.

Red powers her down the runway, closer to the burning wreck and keeps her grounded until the last second. He yanks back and they feel the sudden lift and bank away from the flames. They see the top hatch of the wreck open and a man on fire crawl out, reach his burning hands to the sky, then slip back into the inferno.

"God have mercy," Skeeter mutters, breathing hard.

Dawn awakens the sky as the B-24's zoom over the sea, casting shadows over the water like geese in five V formations. Colonel Jensen pilots the lead plane with his group in fourth position behind Bull Madigan's. Red waves across the span of sky at Denny on the left.

Red gazes out his window at the jewel-blue water below. "I wonder how many ships are sunk down there. How many battles have been fought and forgotten. How many men have died here." He shakes his head. "History will forget what we do today too." He glances at Skeeter and notices he is still pale and shaky.

"Pull yourself together, man. Got a long way to go yet."

He switches on the intercom. "Gunners, test fire when

ready."

The ship clatters from sort bursts of 50-caliber machine guns. A tinge of smoke floats through the ship and smells of burnt cordite gunpowder.

Bull Madigan's group is slowing down. A rift begins to separate his three formations from the two lead groups. The rift widens. Colonel Jensen and the ships behind him have to throttle back to avoid overtaking him. As the formations hit landfall, they turn inland over the island of Corfu. The first two groups pull away at the designated cruising speed and are gone from sight.

Colonel Jensen grabs the flimsy from his radioman and shout into it. "Damn you, Madigan! Move forward at the correct speed! You're dividing us! Move forward now!"

In Madigan's ship, the radioman holds the receiver toward his Colonel. Madigan sits hunched over the controls, his face red and jaw set. He waves the radio away.

Skeeter strains to look ahead, "What the hell's going on?"

"Madigan," Red says. "Decided to do it his way after all."

"What? We're supposed to hit the target at the same time. We're supposed to surprise them so they have no defenses ready. Our bombs are on delay fuses just so we-"

"What do you want me to do? Run him over?" Red snaps. "If Jensen isn't moving, we stay put."

Tex's voice comes over the intercom. "Comin' up on North Albanian Alps. Looks like cloud cover."

They head straight into a thick wall of clouds pegged on the mountain range. Red follows the group up into white oblivion.

"Keep us steady, Tex."

Skeeter is still mumbling to himself. "The first groups' bombs will be going off. We won't have a chance." Red grinds his teeth, wanting to ignore him, knowing he is dead right.

Two groups burst out of the clouds at 15,000 feet like

arrows shot through the white blanket over the Alps.

Madigan's group does not appear.

Colonel Jensen takes the lead and they swoop down the other side of Yugoslavia. Mirrors flash at them from deep in the mountainsides. Red sees the flashing signals.

"Tex, can you read that?"

"V for victory. Must be the Yugoslavian Partisans."

"Hope they're praying for us." Red pulls up tight on the Colonel's formation. Right now he doesn't give a rat's ass where Madigan could be. The damage has already been done. Maybe now Jensen can move them on to the target.

His hopes are dashed when Colonel Jensen leads the two groups in circles, flying a carousel over the brown strip of River Danube.

Skeeter taps the instrument panel nervously. "Now what the hell are we doing?"

"Waiting."

"Wasting precious fuel! This wasn't part of the plan."

Hal comes down from the top turret and checks the gauges. "I hope the Colonel doesn't plan to circle for long. This'll put a dent in the fuel supply." He doesn't seem to notice the effect his words have on Skeeter's nerves. He looks out the window. "Is that the 'Beautiful Blue Danube?' Looks more like a Kansas stream in spring run-off."

"Simple flight plan and the big boys are screwing it up." Red grips the controls, unable to do anything about the anger he feels. "Unbelievable."

Dominick calls over the intercom, "Here he comes now, twelve o'clock."

Madigan's group putters down the mountains and passes them to take the lead.

"Egotistical son-of-a-bitch," Red growls.

The three groups reshape, follow Madigan and drop altitude to zero. They zoom over farmland and Hal continues to press his nose to the window.

"Look at that! Beautiful! I bet nobody goes hungry around here. Looks better than my land."

Red doesn't respond. Sweat glistens on his face as he tries to hold the very heavy ship steady at 200 miles per hour over haystacks and fences. Tex speaks from the intercom. "There goes the 319th. Heading for Steava Romana refinery."

The V of planes in last position separates and speeds to the north. Madigan and Jensen's groups head toward another village in the midst of farmland. Red eases the throttles forward as both groups pick up speed.

"Comin' up on second IP – Targoviste," Tex announces. The village flashes by as Red skims over the church steeple. Skeeter glances at him and sees his white-knuckle grip on the steering. The ground is a blur as Red pushes the throttles harder. Hal silently retreats to the top turret.

"Approaching third IP – Floresti."

The two groups blast over the town, turn northeast and Jensen's moves up next to Madigan's, heading up the train tracks. Twenty-one ships break off and head south. The others quickly reshape formation.

Skeeter looks at the speedometer: 265 MPH.

Tex's voice booms, "That's Deputy Leader going south to Blue Target at Brazi. We're set for White Target."

They approach a cluster of haystacks that pop open like jack-in-the-boxes to reveal 37 mm canon. They belch hot lead as the plane gunners blow them away.

A freight train skims down the tracks. Boxcar sides are kicked off to expose anti-aircraft guns, blasting left and right. Several planes take hits before the gunners strafe the cars.

Gus lines up his sights on the train engine, his expression cool. He shoots and the engine blows sky high, flipping cars into the air. Gus smiles.

Red sees a gauntlet of embanked guns lined up in their path, spewing fire and bullets. He feels his ass squeeze tight as his gunners respond and the plane reverberates.

"You boys are no longer virgins," he shouts into the intercom over the cacophony of explosions. "You're doing a helluva job! Let 'em have it!"

The intercom comes alive with deep-throat howls and whoops as pent-up nerves become steely power.

"Die, Nazi!" Jacob screams.

"Got you, sucker!" Arnie shrieks.

Dominick crawls out of the nose and heads for the bomb bay. Tex slides into his seat in the nose, yanks up the gun and shoots.

"Yeeeeeeehaaaaawww!"

Skeeter sucks in his breath and his face goes ashen as he stares. Colonel Jensen's group heads straight for a tidal wave of fire and smoke. At ten feet off the ground, throttles wide open, they're on a collision course with death.

Madigan must have seen it too. He suddenly veers off and his group follows, completely abandoning their course.

Jensen is seconds away from the black mass and unwavering. His bomb bay doors open and all the other planes loyally following open theirs. They tip up to climb over smoke stacks they can no longer see. Jensen's nose touches the incinerating inferno just as an EXPLOSION blows smoke and fire high into the air. A clear tunnel opens and the group flies over the target.

Antiaircraft cannons blast them.

Red sees the ceiling of smoke sinking back toward them. He looks across formation to Denny's ship. A cannon shell hits Denny's plane. Flame pour out of the waist windows.

"Denny!" Red yells, and stares, unable to do anything for him. "God! No!"

Denny pulls straight up as two parachutes come out on fire and the men drop like rocks. The great plane slides down and explodes into the burning refinery.

Red locks his vision back on formation and grips the wheel as if to crush it in his hands.

"Oh God..." he murmurs. His chest heaves in panic. Skeeter, pale as a ghost, touches him.

"Keep us alive, boss."

Red nods and takes a breath, concentrates on the dance through the smoke stacks, barrage balloons and buildings. Skeeter watches Red's face transform, his cheeks flush, and anger grow in his eyes. He maneuvers the ship like a fighter pilot, leaning slightly forward over the controls, the ship like an extension of his arms, quick and demanding.

Planes blow up around them. Formation is lost and B-24's fly in from different directions.

A plane skids down a street like a rocket with no wings.

Another crashes through three buildings before exploding.

Red is on the intercom. "Let 'em have it, Dom!"

"Bombs away!"

Skeeter and Red feel the lift as 8,000 pounds of bombs drop from their belly.

Steve sits in a mist of burnt cordite and shoots in one direction, swivels and shoots in another. He blows up enemy roof top gunners left and right.

Hal pivots in the top turret, coolly selecting targets and blowing them away.

Gus picks off antiaircraft operators with his eagle eye.

Jacob strafes water tower guns, the blood lust burning in his eyes.

Arnie, in a wild frenzy, shoots embanked machine guns along their path.

Dominick climbs out to the nose guns to join Tex, who calls to Red, "Looks like the higher they fly the more they get shot at. I suggest we stay on deck."

"Will do," Red answers.

Red's right wing snaps a barrage balloon cable, deeply indenting the metal. He tips her completely vertical to zoom between smoke stacks and catches a line of machine gun fire that cuts across her left wing tip like a scythe cutting wheat.

They whip over a building as a 88mm cannon shell rockets from the roof, slams into the flight deck and blows out the other side before it detonates and sprays them with shrapnel. Red and Skeeter glance briefly at the damage, see a lot of sky through the holes as if looking through a sieve, but they fly on, trying to stay alive.

Two wondering B-24's fall into formation with Red's plane, one on either side, as if looking for a leader. But just as suddenly has the tunnel opened, the oily ceiling comes crashing down on top of them. Visibility is suddenly zero. Acrid smoke fills the plane with an oppressive heat and intensity like a forge's fire.

Skeeter coughs and gasps, "We're on instruments."

"Watch them carefully and let's hope we don't hit anybody."

Red and Skeeter slap on oxygen masks. Hairy moments later, while waiting to crash into whatever is out there, they shoot out of the smoke cover, out of the city and across farmland.

The B-24 on the left has disappeared.

Red looks to the right and sees the pilot of the other plane slumped over his controls, flames licking at his back. The plane nosedives into the field and explodes.

They can't think about it for a second, as Skeeter points above them.

"Here comes the Luftwaffe."

Red pulls the ship down until she is barely skimming over fences and rocks. As he struggles to hold her steady, the rest of the crew watches total pandemonium high in the sky over their heads. B-24's race this way and that, some on fire, trying to get away from enemy fighters.

A B-24 dips down to the tree line with a Luftwaffe in hot pursuit, catches a wing in heavy branches and cartwheels across the field, scattering bodies and equipment everywhere.

Red dodges flying plane parts.

Tex calls from the intercom, "Turn 180 degrees south. Let's get out of here."

"Roger."

They scoot over the fields, alone, sneaking under the action above, unnoticed. Red pulls back on the throttles and slows her down. Up ahead he sees a B-24 crash land in a long grass field. The crew hops out and waves as he flies by.

"Poor bastards," Red mutters. "Gonna get shot or end up rotting in some POW camp." Suddenly he is swinging the plane around. "What the hell."

They head straight back at the downed crew.

Red calls, "We're dragging the field. Tex, tell me if it's long enough to land."

Tex's frantic voice yells over the intercom, "Are you crazy? You can't land now! We got a roof full of hornets up there. We got to get out of here!"

"Looks long enough to me. Gear down."

Skeeter stares at him, open mouth. Red glares hard at him, and the copilot drops the landing gear.

"Gunners, watch our ass!"

He banks sharply into the field and he can see the grounded crew cluster together pointing and watching in amazement.

"Full flaps," he orders.

"Roger, full flaps."

A German patrol bursts out of the woods on foot, guns drawn. Hal and Arnie's guns slam them with a wall of bullets that picks them up and tosses them back into the trees.

Red reaches the other end of the field, pulls up in a steep turn, back on the throttles to stalling speed, and drops like a butterfly on the grass. They bump and bounce over the field to the crashed plane.

"Dom, bomb bay open. Arnie, count them as they come in. Get them all."

Hal shouts, "Enemy fighter at 4 o'clock high."

Guns shake the ship.

"We got him!"

The fighter plane falls to the forest and explodes.

They skid to a stop and the grounded crew races for the bomb bay doors.

"All ten aboard!" Arnie calls.

"Roger," Red says. "Let's go! Flaps up."

He whips the plane around and taxies at high speed. "When we hit 80, give me full flaps."

"Roger."

The heavy ship careens toward the tree line with a 4,000 horsepower roar.

Skeeter watches the trees fast approaching with wide eyes. "80, full flaps." They feel the lift as the wheels leave the grass.

"Gear up."

"Roger."

Skeeter closes his eyes as his window fills with a wall of trees.

"Come on, Betsy!" Red groans. He yanks the stick back in his lap and they soar up, clipping branches with metallic thuds. On they fly, leveling off at ground zero.

"Milk the flaps up slow," Red instructs.

"Roger." Skeeter tries to fill his constricted lungs and to breathe again. Red sighs and wipes the sweat from his face.

"Tex, give us a heading for Corfu. We're flying solo now. Stay sharp, boys. Don't want to get in any Luftwaffe's cross-hairs."

Tex's voice says, "206 degrees."

"Roger."

Steve shouts on the intercom, "Enemy fighter at 5 o'clock!" As the ship's guns clatter, Red tips on the tattered left wing and swings the bomber in a tight turn. The fighter pilot is caught in his own momentum and plows into the field, flinging debris everywhere.

Red pulls out of the turn over the burning wreck and flies on.

Skeeter shakes his head as some of the color returns to his face. "I've never seen anyone fly a bomber like a Piper Cub. Damn."

"Hal, check our fuel," says Red. "Calculate if we have

enough." Hal ducks in to check the gauges.

"We're at twelve-fifty. It'll be real close."

"Check again near Malta and we'll make a decision then."

The rescued pilot enters the flight deck and stride over to Red with a huge grin on his blond, good-looking face. He is in his early thirties, athletic and lean as if he ran track for years. He slaps Red on the back and laughs like a man who has just been given a new chance to live.

"You're a goddamn genius! Man, I don't if I should kiss you or kneel at your feet! How much do I owe you for that stunt?"

"How much ya got?" Red asks with a grin while he stays focused on flying.

Don puts both hands on Red's shoulders and gives him a heart-felt squeeze. "Not enough. It would never be enough. I couldn't repay what you did for us, the risk you took."

Red shrugs, "Don't worry about it. You'll just be under obligation to me for the rest of your life. Say hi to Skeeter here. He's the brains of this operation and I get all the credit."

Don extends an arm to Skeeter's shoulder. "Hi, Skeeter. Fabulous to meet you. You guys are really the most amazing pair. What's his name?"

"Crazy Red, or something like that. And who are you?"

"Don Peterson of the 93rd at your service," he says, bowing humbly between them. "Why are you guys hedgehopping?"

"Survival," Red explains. "Staying out of the action at 5,000 feet. Pull up that jump seat and sit a spell."

"Thanks." Don obliges, sitting just behind Red. They fly into the mountains and head on tilted wings up canyons and through ravines. Other B-24's struggle to make it over the range, some with parts of wings and tails shot off, some on three engines. One plane coughs and sputters, smoking. It turns away, back to flat country. Nine parachutes bloom out of it, not ten.

Betsy floats over the mountains and down toward the Eonian Sea.

The three men gaze out over a sparkling, unmarred world.

The picturesque beauty strives to wipe out the horrors of a war they have just left behind. None of them, sitting there in awe for having survived, can comprehend how the world can be full of so many hypocrisies.

"Tex," Red speaks softly into the intercom. "Give us a heading for home base."

"New heading, 172 degrees."

"Roger." Red pauses, feeling the silence of the humming ship, knowing that each boy on board has become a man in the face of his first and most formidable fight. They are all quiet in their shock.

"How's it going back there in the waist," Red asks on intercom. "Kind of breezy with all the holes?"

Arnie answers, "What holes? Thought it was a new air conditioning system."

"How are our guests back there?"

"Great! Some are asleep, some are asking for a bottle of Scotch and a deck of cards. Some want to know where the girls are." Arnie laughs into the intercom. "Told 'em I don't have my business license yet."

Don chuckles and shakes his head. "Too damn much, you guys."

Red takes the ship out over the water and lowers until her belly skims the waves. The thrill of zooming over open ocean, alone, with nothing else in sight, amazes them all.

"You like it down here, don't you?" Don asks quietly.

Skeeter nudges Don and they look up to 6,000 feet and see a dozen B-24's flying parallel. As they watch, six ME-109 German fighters swoop in and buzz circles around them before attacking. Like ringside spectators, they hear the boom and ratatata of guns as the fighters take diving passes at the big birds. One by one, four bombers stagger, smoke and burst into flames and fall to sea. Three of the Germans are shredded to pieces by bomber guns. The rest break off and fly back to hell.

"Yeah," Red says, "I like it down here."

Tex calculates at his desk and leans into the intercom. “About two and a half hours from base. Make a decision: Malta or Benghazi.”

Hal interjects, “Maybe there’re two and a half hours left of fuel, give or take a cup or less. How lucky do you all feel?”

“Lucky enough,” Red answers. “Let’s go to Benghazi.”

They can hear Tex sigh across the wires, “Roger.”

Red sinks deeper into his seat and stares straight ahead. Fatigue lends a tremor to his arms and hands on the wheel. Don squeezes his shoulder, waking him from his revere.

“You ok?”

Red swallows, blinks. “Lost a good friend over the target.”

Don nods, “I’m sorry. I know what that’s like.”

“I saw it happen,” Red says between his clamped teeth. “Poor bastard didn’t have a chance. It’s over for him. He'll never see his kids or his wife again. They’ll bury an empty casket.”

They fall silent and listen to nothing but the steady drone of the engines. Like a lone swan floating home, Betsy heads for the coast of Africa. Sun sinks into the western sea and glints off of her mottled skin. They put miles between them and the dead they leave behind.

Hal enters the flight deck. “Fuel’s on empty.” He looks at the men expectantly, anxiety tightening his face.

“Everybody think levitation,” Red says. “If that doesn’t work, get ready to swim.”

Skeeter points, “There’s the beach!”

An engine coughs then quits. Red’s hands move quickly over the controls. “Feathering the prop. Boost power to the others. Come on, Betsy. Give us a little more.”

Hal stares out the window at the distant runway, fast approaching. He closes his eyes and it looks like he’s praying.

Another engine quits.

Red pushes throttles to the firewall, tries to keep the ship in the air. Don quietly, calmly observes.

"Gear down," Red says. "Full flaps."

"Roger."

Red grabs the radio and switches to the control tower. "Forty four control, this is four-twenty-one, coming in on two engines."

Tower answers, "Four-twenty-one clear to land. Over."

Betsy sputters at the head of the runway just as all engines fail, and settles to the ground like a bird on a lake.

Red tries the brakes. Nothing. Hal grabs hold of the side and clings for dear life. "Skeeter, try the hand brakes!" Red orders. Skeeter pumps madly on the brakes as the ship eats up ground, careening down the runway. The brakes suddenly catch and Red slows her steadily until she stops at the very end. The whole ship echoes with cheering.

Don grins and slaps Red's back. "By God, we're on the ground, and in one piece!"

Red glances at his watch, "Fourteen hours and seven minutes."

Hal bounds out of the flight deck. Don and Skeeter stand up to leave. Fatigue, deep and deadening, washes over Red and he slumps over the wheel. Don takes his arm.

"You've been there a long time, my friend."

Red nods, "About a thousand years." Red tries to stand and his legs buckle. Don catches and steadies him.

The two crews exit the plane as Corporal Hammon speeds up in the transport truck. Colonel Jensen is seated beside him. Both men stare at the number of fly boys dropping out of Betsy's belly.

Hammon almost spits out his whole wad. "I'll be damned!"

Jensen points at Skeeter. "How the hell many people did you take on this mission?"

"Ten, sir."

Red and Don, last out of the plane, approach the truck. "Let me explain, sir," Red says. "We picked them up hitch hiking.

Figured we couldn't just leave them there."

Jensen peers at the guest pilot. "Don Peterson? Colonel Don Peterson of the 93rd? Is that you?"

"Yessir," Don grins. Red turns to him with a look of surprise.

"You're a Colonel?"

"Yes indeed," Don pounds Red's back. "And a very happy one at that!"

"How the hell did you do that, Red?" Jensen looks back and forth between them, confused.

"Well, sir," Red begins, dropping an arm around Don's shoulders. "I figure you got a good deal. We dropped our bombs on target. My gunners took out German fighters. We left with ten and came back with twenty. All in a day's work."

Colonel Jensen wipes his face and shakes his head. "Hop in. Let's get you to Interrogation and hear the whole crazy story." He turns to Don. "I've got to call the 93rd and tell them you're alive. I'll let them know you were picked up by Crazy Red himself."

They pile into the truck and take off as darkness falls.

4

Red tosses back and forth on his cot under mosquito netting. Outside the wind moans and hisses through the skeleton of the German wreck. The sound becomes the scream of anti-aircraft missiles in his dream. Ships blow up in blinding flashes. Burning men reach out for help.

Denny's eyes stare and his mouth moves as he falls into the flames, falling, falling, burning until his words finally echo out. "You promised!"

Red wakes with a gasp, sweating, his eyes wide and his hands pressed over his ears as if to shut out the words.

Whitie and Lowel circle the plane. Whitie whistles. "Our pretty lady ain't so pretty any more."

"She tainted," Lowel shakes his head sadly.

Whitie pats her nose and examines her shredded, dented wing tips. "What did they do to you, baby?"

"Look at this!" Lowel reaches for a hole in her skin and pulls out a bird's nest, with tufts of hay and branches. His eyes twinkle. "Maybe hedgehopping is better than sex."

Whitie snorts, "More like ground-sliding!"

Bob comes out of the plane as Red and the crew enter the hardstand. "I never seen a luckier crew. One of the control cables is spliced. If it'd snapped you wouldn't be here. And all those holes! That rocket shot right between Gus and Jacob's stations. Unbelievable."

Gus murmurs, "God's watching over us."

"Yeah, and we only have 24 more missions to fly," Mike says. They all turn and look at him. Moment of silence as the truth sets in.

Red breaks the tension. "We'll leave you guys to the fixin'

up."

"And it'll take a while," Bob says. "Got to give ol' Betsy a face lift."

Whitie sobs loudly, clinging to her nose. "She'll never be beautiful again!" Lowel consoles him with a pat on the back.

Bob rubs a hand over her too. "Well, at least you guys are all back safe."

"Thanks, Bob," Red says sarcastically. "Good to know you care about us more than Betsy." He grabs Bob in a bear hug and kisses his stubby cheek. Bob shoves him away gruffly and hastily retreats inside the plane, while the crew laughs.

The Chaplain sorts through a large pile of billfolds, photos, and letters on a table. His shoulders are slumped and his hands move mechanically, his eyes downcast. Red and the crew watch in reverent quiet as he separates the unclaimed personals.

"Depressing," Red comments. Chaplain's eyes raise and lock onto Red's. Waves of pain ride through them.

"I love my calling," the young clergy says in a voice stifled in sorrow. "I love every one of these men. Then there's a mission and some don't come back. Another life is sacrificed. Why? Can't they see how hate destroys us? It snuffs out lives with violence and leaves nothing but heartache and suffering. Why do we choose this? What is wrong with mankind?"

He slides their billfolds across the table and turns away, too overwhelmed to speak.

"I'll be writing to Denny Wilson's family," Red touches his arm softly. "That's one letter you won't have to write. I'll take care of it."

Chaplain simply nods, no longer facing them, and the crew quietly files out.

Darkness falls among the tents. Red sits on his cot and caps his pen, running his finger over the envelope he has just addressed: To Janet Wilson, 233 El Camino Real, San Diego, CA.

The cool breeze enters through the open flaps and he sees several crews setting up for a campfire outside. Not only his boys, but other crews have come to join them, all fighting the feeling of loneliness. Bottles of something soothing pass between them.

Red leaves the envelope on his cot and steps out to the center of camp. The crewmen settle on the sand and watch Tex start a fire with flint and steel, like a cowboy on the prairie.

"I never seen anyone do that before, except in the movies," Arnie says with great admiration.

"Watch and learn, boys," Tex says.

"A match would have been faster," Jacob scoffs.

A crewman, lounging in the sand, sees Red and waves him over. "Hey, Crazy Red, pick up any hitch hikers lately?"

Red grabs his crotch. "Just General Rinky Dink here." They all laugh raucously, already lubricated with alcohol. Red moves around the periphery of men, watching Tex's fire take on the chunks of wood with gusto. The cowboy steps back and solemnly puts his flint and steel in their leather pouch, as the others nod their approval. Red too admires the Texan, not just for his camping skills, but for the nerves of steel he demonstrated on the mission.

It takes going through a battle to know what kind of men you have. I've got the best, Red smiles to himself. He continues to move around until he hears something coming from one of the tents. He steps closer, away from the noisy circle of men, and hears soft voices and hiccupping sobs coming from Gus' tent. He leans near the flaps.

"It's God's will," Gus says in a calming voice. "Accept it."

Jimmie sounds strangled with tears. "They're going to haunt me forever. I should have been with them."

"No, you were meant to live." Gus must be patting his back. "You're a crack shot and another crew will need you."

"Captain Wilson was like a big brother to me. He made me stay in the infirmary when I could have gone."

"You had to obey orders. There was nothing else you

could do. You need to let it go and carry on now. He would have wanted you to."

More muffled sobs, and Red moves quietly away, back to the men at the fire that burns brightly, reflecting off their less than sober faces.

Tex sits on his haunches and stares at the flames, the Stetson casting a shadow over his eyes. "He should be strung up and quartered. A lot of fuel was wasted waiting for him."

Dominick nods, "And the enemy was waiting like a spider for a fly." Men grumble their agreement and despite the alcohol, nothing can wipe the pain and horror from their minds' eyes. They have all seen too much too soon and will never forget a moment of it.

A crewman says, "Bull Madigan ain't the only one responsible for the mess. I heard the lead group took a wrong turn after the second IP and when they figured it out they hurried up to the refinery and lost formation."

Two other crewmen sit up, cheeks burning and indignant. One says, "That's because the lead plane saw the resistance and hightailed it back here."

"Fully loaded?" Tex asks.

"Yeah."

Groans of incredulity rise from the circle. The first crewman huffs, "So the rest of the group flew around bombing whatever they could see."

Hal shakes his head, "Damn inferno when we got there."

"The delay triggers on the bombs worked against us," Dominick adds. "They just kept blowing up in front of us."

"Court martial those sons-of-bitches, " Tex growls.

The crewman snorts derisively, "They'll never touch them. You're lucky to have Jensen. The rest of them cover each others' asses. Welcome to the politics of war."

Red retreats to his tent. He's had enough. Maybe if he puts the pillow over his head he'll be able to sleep. *No dreams, please God, not tonight.*

Next day, Tex drags himself out of his tent, looking wasted. "Damn I need a beer." He stumbles up to Red who waits in the shadow of the German wreck. Tex hangs on to a jutting piece and closes his eyes. Red watches as the rest of the crew assembles slowly. Steve, Mike and Hal now wear the Jacob-fashion, T-shirt-over-head-and-neck style against the rising, heating sun. Arnie shows up wearing a German pith helmet, complete with a bullet hole through the front.

"Where'd you get that?" Jacob asks harshly.

"Traded for it last night," Arnie replies gleefully.

"Take it off!"

"Like hell I will!" Arnie backs away defensively. Hal grabs Jacob as he lunges at Arnie.

"Relax," Hal clings to struggling Jacob. "It's just a hat, for the sun."

But Jacob won't be calmed. He spits angrily at Arnie. "How can you call yourself a Jew?"

"Cool it, man," Arnie moves by him, pointing a finger. "You'll get an ulcer."

Red steps in, "That's enough. Back off both of you." He glares challengingly at them until Hal releases Jacob who gruffly straightens himself out, and Arnie saunters away. Gus approaches the group with Jimmie in tow. They look like the picture of Air Force men, attired in proper uniforms, not the sloppy T-shirts and rumpled pants of the others. Gus steps close to Red and speaks softly.

"Can Jimmie hang out with us?"

"Of course," Red says. "More the merrier. I was just about to tell these knuckleheads about my idea for the day."

They all gaze at him expectantly, savoring the memory of their beach day. They've all learned to appreciate Red's ideas.

"What say we head for the Bazaar in Benghazi?"

"Are we allowed to do that?" Mike asks.

Tex shoves him, "Shut up, boy. You ruin a good plan."

"Any one of you is welcome to stay here," Red continues.

"I, for one, am headed for some adventure. Suit yourselves." He marches away and they all fall in quickly behind him.

Corporal Hammon, in his usual form, zooms along the desert road, clearing his throat to spew a load and leave a long, brown mark on the sand. He grins at Red. "Wish I could go with ya."

"How do we get into the city?"

Hammon pats Red's leg and winks. "I'll take you around back. Avoid the MP's stationed by the front gates."

"Thank you, my man. You're very resourceful." That comment has Hammon gurgling in his seat.

The crew wanders into the city along a narrow, cobbled street. Many buildings, houses and shops are gutted and half-toppled, as if they were caught in the crossfire of one of many wars. No one seems to have tried to repair anything. Where rubble is strewn in the streets, people have simply walked a path around it. As if no one believes the destruction will ever end, or perhaps they are so jaded by endless fighting, they don't pick up the pieces and the city looks as if were crumbling around them.

The deeper the crew penetrates the city, the more crowded and noisy the street life becomes. Open doors and windows and some missing walls give glimpses into Arab homes where women and children freeze and stare back at them, fear in their eyes.

Overwhelming odors of cooking spices mix with the street stench of donkey dung and urine as Arab men push by, pulling animals or sitting in groups at corners.

The crew walks slowly along, unconsciously crammed close together. Their boyhood innocence shows as they gawk at the filthy, teaming streets. They let Red take the lead and he moves along, getting bumped by his charges every time he slows down. They pass a doorstep where a boy sits, tossing a ball. He jumps up and runs after them.

"You want guide?" he calls in a high-pitched voice. The

group stops, clustered together like chicks against their hen. The boy is small and thin, making him look younger than his thirteen or fourteen years. He is dressed in Arab pants with a faded British Army jacket, with dirty sandaled feet. His malnourished face is framed by tussled black hair, and his black eyes look sharp as they size up the Americans.

"I take, you want to go. Show you good places. Safe with me."

Red looks from the boy to the crew. Skeeter shrugs. Dominick nods.

"Can't hurt," Tex says.

Red faces the boy and frowns to show he is not fooling around. "You take us around. Safe, good places. The market."

The boy grins and waves them to follow. He trots off down the street. The crew hurries to catch up, moving as one. They follow him into even more crowded, more commercial streets filled with men, animals, and venders selling wares out of carts. They gape at the sights, wrinkling noses at the pungent smells, and hopping over piles of manure. They defensively keep their backs together.

Their guide takes them down a narrow, shadowy street, danker and dirtier even than the others. Here women of every mixture of race stand in crumbling doorways, dressed in dirty rags that reveal the tools of their trade. Some smile with toothless, wide mouths, some stand rigid, eyes downcast. They all gesture to the Americans, inviting them to step off the street into the dark holes behind them.

"You like?" the boy holds his hands up as if offering them all of these poor creatures at once. The crew presses up against a barren wall as Arab men and native soldiers stagger out of the brothels in various degrees of drunk.

"No," Red scolds the boy. "We don't want this."

The boy frowns up at him, utterly confused. He tilts his small head as if thinking. He must have gotten an idea, as he suddenly snaps his finger and smiles knowingly.

"You want little girl."

He makes hand signs for someone smaller than himself and moves his hips as if having sex. "I take you my sister. Nice. Small." The crew watches the pathetic display and groans in horror.

"Let's ditch this kid," Tex suggests. Hal and Mike are gazing at the women, and their faces are flushed red.

"I don't think we should be here," Mikes says.

Red grabs the boy's arm. "We want shops." He points to his eyes and turns his head in an exaggerated gesture. "We want to look around and see what merchants are selling."

The boy looks around the group in dismay. "You no want girls?"

"NO!" the whole crew shouts at once. He sighs mightily, as if finding it difficult to please these weird men.

"Come," he signals them to follow.

As they leave the street, Gus and Jimmie who trail behind, notice two Arabs emerge from the shadows. Turbans and thick beards cloak their faces, yet the glint of steely eyes catches Gus and Jimmie's attention, and the sudden shine of curved swords on their belts. The two crewmen hurry to stay close to the others.

The boys leads them up a street choked with pedestrians and venders to an equally congested plaza with every imaginable product for sale on stands, on the cobblestones, in little shops that completely surround the area. The noise of bleating animals, shouting men, hooves on stone, sing-song venders calling to buy, buffet the crew. They stand, pressed together, as an island in the sea of humanity.

Gus nudges Jimmie, signals with his chin. They've been followed. The two Arabs hang back about 50 meters, but do not hide.

The boy gathers the crew in a huddle. "You want buy. He-sells he say two times right price. He say 'last price'. You say half. He mad. You say little more. Ok. He happy, right price." He admonishes them with a finger. "You pay first price, he-sells no respect you."

Red nods. "Alright. Everyone understands how to play the game, right?" He looks around for agreement. "Let's break into pairs and meet back here in an hour. Do not lose sight of your partner. One hour." They all glance at watches and Red hands the boy money, which instantly disappears into his British jacket. "You come back and take us out of here and I'll give you more then."

The boy grins, backs up and melts into the crowd. Red watches the crew pair off and wade into the Bazaar like fish out of water, Dominick with Tex, Hal with Mike, and Gus with Jimmie. Arnie tries to join Jacob and Steve.

"No way!" Jacob snaps at him. "Not while you're wearing that damn helmet."

Tex steps between them. "Come on with us, Arnie. Leave the girls to fret."

They wander off, leaving Skeeter and Red to wind through the narrow path between shops and stands. Venders shout at them, shove products at them aggressively, anything from cloth to plucked chicken carcasses. "Hey, Johnny!" they call to the Americans. "Look! Cheap!"

Skeeter hangs close to Red. He flinches at the noise.

"See anything you like?" Red asks.

They pass through a section of scarves, jewelry and incense.

"Hell, I don't know," Skeeter says, looking cautiously around and bumping into Red.

"You ought to get something nice for Suzie." He holds up a beautiful shawl of translucent blue material that feels like silk and bares intricate embroidery. Skeeter's eyes light up as Red holds it in the sun, watching it shimmer warmly. "Here you go. Make her your harem princess."

Skeeter tentatively touches the fabric as if afraid to ruin it. His mouth forms an *ah* of delight. "Sure is pretty. But when would she wear something Arab?"

Red winks at him, "You have her wear nothing but this on your wedding night."

A mischievous grin steals across the boy's face. They turn to the vender, but then Red spots a bolt of delicate aqua silk lying on a crowded table. It is interwoven with silver threads and graceful silver leaves that glow in a startling pattern.

The merchant sidles up to them, hawk-eyed and shrewd under the turban and above the thick beard. "You like, Johnny?"

Red shrugs, noncommittal. The merchant lays a stretch of the material over Red's hands. It is breathtaking, but Red shows nothing in his face. He forces himself to look away as if bored.

"One meter – one pound," The merchant demands. Red quickly calculates, that means four American dollars. He musters all of his acting ability to shake his head in shock and back away. Skeeter slips to the side, watching but staying out of this.

"Too much!" Red scowls.

The merchant slips up closer, looks around, as if afraid to be overheard, and whispers, "Last price?"

Red considers, "Three meters for a pound."

The merchant grabs his heart as if in cardiac arrest. He flings himself about the shop in a magnificent performance of victimized abuse. His turban threatens to fall off and he yanks at his beard, closing his eyes in agony. Red admires the act. Skeeter cringes into the bolts of fabric, trying to hide.

Finally Red says, "Last price?"

The merchant freezes in mid-fling. "Three meters, 2 pounds." Red laughs, tapping his head as if the Arab were crazy. "Last price?" he asks sweetly.

Red steps up to him, getting in his face, his green eyes fierce. His taps a hard finger on the merchant's chest. "Three meters, and the scarf, 2 pounds. Last, last, last price."

The merchant smiles, pleased. "Ok." He measures three meters of the spectacular material, wraps it in brown paper and wraps Skeeter's scarf. Red hands him two Libyan pounds.

The merchant is now warm and congenial. "How your hair be that color?"

"My mother gave it to me."

The merchant breathes in awe. "I never see this color."

Red bends forward and lets the man pet his head. He sees a small, curve blade knife with a carved handle on the table. He picks it up and slices several locks of hair onto a piece of wrapping paper. He grins. "For you, baksheesh." Red and Skeeter take their purchases and head for the street.

"Johnny, you fine man," the merchant stops them and reverently places the little dagger in Red's hand. "For you, baksheesh."

They smile at each other.

Skeeter clutches his package and waits with Red as the rest of the crew wanders back to their meeting place. Several of them carry wrapped packages, but Gus and Jimmie are empty-handed, and Jacob looks disgusted, his hands in his pockets.

"Filthy Arabs," he mutters.

The guide boy suddenly materializes and motions them to follow. He takes them on a new route toward the other end of town. He seems edgy and glances around, waving his hand for them to follow quickly.

"You leave fast," he whispers to Red.

"What's wrong?"

The boy looks at him, hesitates. "American enemies." He leads them on without another word. Gus and Jimmie take up the rear and catch glimpses of the two sword-wielding Arabs following, but maintaining a distance.

Moments later they arrive at the city's front gates. The boy halts and points to the American MP's standing guard outside.

"You go now," he says with a shooing motion.

Red hands him money. "You did a good job. Thank you."

A brief smile flashes over the boy's small features and he leans close. Red leans down to his level. "Careful of enemies." He touches Red's hair in a quick gesture and scampers down the narrow street. Coming from the other direction are four Arabs armed with swords. Gus and Jimmie push the others out the gates. The crew waltzes by the MP's. They wave and smile. The

MP's shout, "Hey!" but there is nothing they can do, so the crew heads back to the base.

The crew sits on crates, eating the hashed-mashed C-rations. Tex sits close to the men who attended his campfire last night. One crewman says, "Some of the boys went out last night and did some vigilante action."

"What do you mean?" Tex asks, pausing as he eats to level his eyes on the man.

"You didn't hear about that American those Arabs cut up a couple of weeks ago?

Tex nods, "Yeah, I heard."

"Well, some of us aren't going to hang around and take it."

Another young man lowers his voice to add, "They shot some syphilis-ridden Arabs on donkeys. Sent the rest of the scum a message. Don't mess with us."

Tex lowers his head, the Stetson covering his face. "Y'all may have stirred them up more than stopped 'em. Dangerous to play with the enemy on their own turf. Like the Indians, you know? Peace treaties and all that. You have no idea what these Arabs are liable to do."

The two crewmen snort indignantly. One pats his service pistol on his belt. "Let 'em try it. We'll be waiting."

Tex peers at them from under his hat. Their youthful, sun burnt faces and total ignorance make him lose his appetite. He dumps the rest of the slop in the sand, covers it with his boot and walks away.

Red and the crew head for the hardstand.

"No Jimmie this morning?" Red asks Gus who shuffles along alone.

"Nope," he answers in his melancholy way. "Said he's going to see if he's been reassigned. Then he's going target practicing."

Red pats the boy's back. "It'd be good for him to get a new home soon." Gus nods.

Lowel and Whitie sit on top of the plane, welding patches over the holes. Bob comes out of her belly.

"Well, well, finally decided to come work?" he admonishes the crew. "We thought you'd left yesterday to look for more hitch hikers."

"We had business at the Bazaar in Benghazi," Red says as he turns to the crew. "Ok, boys, go see to your stations." They all clamor into the ship. Red hangs back.

"You aren't part of those vigilantes, are you?" Bob frowns. "You stayed away from those women like I told you?"

"I heard something about that," Red shakes his head. "Foolishness, if you ask me. And no, we just went to look around, do a little shopping."

"Stay away from them Arabs, I tell you. There's going to be trouble on account of those foolhardy boys, you'll see. They're gonna be sorry they messed with the hornet's nest. You stay clear of it."

"Yes, mother dear."

Bob shakes a fat finger at him. "I'm better than a mother to you right now, so you best be listening. Besides, we're all heading for England pretty soon anyway."

"England?"

Bob props his hands on his hips under the greasy coveralls, throws his head back with pride that he knows the inside scoop. "Going to move the whole 44th. You boys'll find out tonight when they tell everybody. Move out in a day or two."

Red looks at him suspiciously. "How did you get this privileged information?"

Bob grins. "I got ears everywhere." Red laughs and heads inside the plane.

Late afternoon and the dunes cast lengthening shadows over the sand. Jimmie stands alone, down in a pocket between dunes, aiming his scope hunting rifle and fires into the opposite sand wall. Like a cracking whip, the sound echoes over the desert. Jimmie concentrates on a point he has targeted, totally consumed with his marksmanship. If he had stopped and looked around, perhaps he would have noticed that it was late and he was vulnerable, out away from base by himself. But Jimmie has a one-track mind and right now he is improving his shooting score. He stops momentarily to reload, his ears ringing dully.

He never sees the four Arabs crawling on their bellies to the top of the dune behind him. He doesn't hear them stand up, draw their swords and charge down on him. What he feels is the first slash of a blade through his body and only manages to yelp once before he is cut to pieces.

Red and the crew head for the slop line at dusk. They see Corporal Hammon zoom by in a jeep. Red waves and Hammon slams on the brakes and slides up to him in a cloud of dust.

"What's your hurry, Corporal?" Then he sees Hammon's face, sick with terror. His mouth hangs open, tobaccoless and for once he enunciates clearly.

"Just saw it. Saw it with my own eyes. Got to get him the news. Got to tell the Colonel." He sweats, his hands shaking. Red and the crew gather around the jeep.

"It was a mess, I tell ya. Horrible. Never in all my days seen anything like it. Got to tell the Colonel." His mouth is flapping slack on his shocked face.

"What, Corporal? What happened? What did you see?" Red tries to get him to focus. The crew gathers around to listen.

"That boy you had with you guys yesterday. Was it just yesterday? Oh my God..." he rubs a hand over his eyes as if to wipe away the image.

Gus pushes the others out of his way and grabs Hammon's arm, shakes him. "Jimmie? What about him?"

Hammon stares at Gus with haunted eyes. "They killed him. Hacked him to pieces. I seen it. Our men're trying to get what's left on a stretcher and bring him in. Target practicing. He was out there alone. Dear Lord." Hammon slaps Gus' hand off him and puts the jeep in gear. "Got to tell the Colonel." Tires kick up a cloud as his spins away.

Gus looks like he's been punched. He drops his mess kit as his chest contracts. Everyone is frozen, watching him. Suddenly he turns and dashes back to tent city.

It's a bright, shadowless desert night of utter silence. Red and the crew carry their service pistols in hand as they follow a lone figure running out across the sand with a hunting rifle. They keep their distance from Gus, yet keep him in sight.

Gus arrives at the target practice dunes and halts. Blood, shreds of flesh, and cloth in a two-meter radius cover the sand in black splotches. The puddles reflect moonlight wetly.

Gus drops to his knees and vomits. He is shaking as he heaves. Then he grips the rifle hard. He glances at it as if to strengthen his resolve. Slowly he gets up and begins to walk around the gore, studying the ground with the expert eye of a true hunter.

Red and the others watch from a dune above him. They see him break into a trot over the desert, his head down, watching prints.

"He's tracking 'em like elk in the Minnesota woods," Tex whispers.

Red signals them to follow. "Let's keep him in sight, boys."

They swing wide around the splattered sand and jog after Gus.

Sweat glistens off the jogging men in the moonlight. An hour has passed and they keep moving steadily on. Suddenly Red holds up his hand and they all stop and drop to the ground. Half a kilometer away they see Gus crouching low as he approaches a hollow in the desert floor glowing brightly with campfire light.

Four Arabs sit around the fire, speaking softly. One lights a cigar-size joint with an ember and lays back, puffing. He hands it to another who says something and they all chuckle. Another picks up pieces of cloth from a bloody pile, what is left of an American uniform, and feeds them slowly into the flames.

One of the Arabs holds Jimmie's rifle in the firelight. He moves his hands over the workmanship and comments on the quality. He puts his eye to the scope and looks around. He freezes. The other bearded men follow his gaze as his lowers the scope.

Gus stands at the top of the hollow. Patiently he waits for everyone's attention. They jump to their feet and grab up swords. One shouts at the Arab holding the rifle. Too late.

Gus shoots a 45 slug into his head, blowing it up like a watermelon. Jimmie's rifle flies out of the firelight. Gus pauses, letting the three others think about it.

"Go to hell!" his voice thunders over the expanse of sands.

They charge at him, swords high. BOOM! An Arab tumbles backward, a slug between the eyes.

In slow motion, Gus drops the rifle. They rush up at him. Cool as if on a turkey shoot, he draws his pistol, blasts a man in the face. The last one runs at him like a steam engine, breathing hard, his dark features twisted with rage, the sword arm poised high above him. He rushes within range and brings the sword slashing down.

Gus steps inside the swing of his enemy's arm, blocks it with his left elbow and shoots him in the throat. The Arab's eyes widen as he stumbles over, spraying blood like a hydrant over Gus and out over the sand.

Red and the crew come to a skidding halt at the top of the hollow. They look down to see Gus standing among the bodies, blood splattered. He turns and looks at them, his face a grotesque bloody mask. Any semblance of the boy-Gus they knew is gone. He turns his back on them, holsters his pistol and begins to drag each body to the campfire.

Tex steps forward as if to assist him. Red puts a hand out to stop him, shakes his head, no. They continue to stand there and watch.

Methodically Gus picks up each sword, poises it over each chest of the dead, finds a space between ribs and slams it through each heart. He takes a piece of bloody uniform that once belonged to his friend, lights it in the fire and set the hair, beard and clothing on fire of each skewered body. He walks out of the bonfire light to retrieve Jimmie's rifle, picks up his own, and calmly starts walking out across the desert, heading for base.

The crew exchanges glances, but no one says a word. They follow him back to base.

5

Red's crew joins the exodus of airmen, duffel bags over shoulders, abandoning the tents and heading for the hardstands.

Gus walks a few paces behind and utters not a word from his hardened jaws. His eyes are down cast and the crew gives him room to breathe. They walk in somber silence until Tex drops back and puts an arm around Gus' shoulders and pulls him up to the group.

Arnie, minus the German helmet, nudges Steve. "Did you hear about the English girls? They love American fly boys and they know all kinds of tricks in the hay."

"Are you planning to learn a few tricks for your whorehouse?" Steve smirks.

Arnie shoves him, frowning as if offended. "It ain't gonna be no he-whore house. The girls got to know the tricks."

Steve rolls his eyes. Hal gets a dreamy look on his pudgy round face. "I like mine country fresh, like love and marriage."

"That's right," Mike concurs. "Nothing commercial for me."

Arnie makes derisive noises and waves his free hand. "You don't get it, boys, do you? Why buy the cow when milk is so cheap?" Steve joins in Arnie's laughter. The two pinch Hal's cheeks.

"You're so naïve!" Arnie pretends to kiss him. Hal tosses him off.

The crew slogs along, sweating in the morning heat under heavy duffel bags. Nobody says anything for a while, though the camaraderie would at least distract them away from the images that in so short a time have blazoned in their minds. They have seen more death in horrible, unspeakable ways than most people see in a lifetime. Each of them has to deal with it or tuck it away somewhere because they are at war and war stops for no one.

Skeeter walks close to Red. "I hear the missions out of England are tough." Before Red can reply, Jacob butts in with his usual sharp tongue.

"Why did you sign up for this war if you're afraid to fight?"

Skeeter glances back at him frowning. "Didn't say I was afraid! I just heard is all."

"Quit listening to the jerks," Jacob dismissing caustically.

Dominick steps up to defend Skeeter. "Lay off him, Jacob. We all hear things. We're all scared sometimes. You're scared too, I'll bet. Plenty, or you won't have to bully somebody else."

"Kiss my ass," Jacob spits back.

"Mark the spot! You're all ass to me."

Red halts the group and stares at each one of their heat-flushed faces. They all look back at him and know they've pushed too far. "Knock it off you guys. We're all feeling it. But we're a crew. We watch out for each other. The guy you piss off today may save your life tomorrow. So cut the bullshit."

He walks on and the others follow, chagrined. Jacob reaches out and pats Skeeter's back. Dominick puts his arm around Jacob. "Maybe you're not all ass."

Jacob cracks a grin and punches him.

Red leans out his window and calls to Bob. "Want a ride to England with us?"

Bob shakes his head, "Nope. People will think you been picking up hitchhikers again. C-47's are on their way to get us. We'll probably beat you there."

"Hell, you haven't seen what I can do with good ol' Miss Betsy. No C-47 will pass her up."

Bob grins hugely, showing his missing tooth. "You've got to stop in Marrakech to gas up. Just don't get stuck there with all those Moroccan girls."

"Who me? Girls? Never!" Red laughs and waves.

Betsy zooms down the runway. Red turns her sharply back toward base. "Gear up." He flips on the intercom. "Let's say good-by in style, boys."

Tex's voice reaches them. "I was afraid of that! Hang on everybody!"

With full throttles and a mighty ROAR, Red drops her to three feet above the ground and heads straight for Bob, Whitie and Lowel who stand there as if confused for a moment. Then they dive spread-eagle to the ground. They press hands to their ears as 4,800 horsepower booms over their heads.

Betsy turns with her wing almost touching the ground and kicks up a huge dust cloud.

Colonel Jensen steps out of the Headquarters building, hearing the low-flying plane. Betsy screams by him and Jensen catches a glimpse of Red's salute. Jensen grins and salutes back.

"Crazy Red," he mutters.

Betsy takes off from Marrakech airbase and flies low over the old walled city of Median with its whitewashed balconies and palm tree-lined streets. The big bird flies out over the water at 200 feet.

The crew moves about, setting themselves up for the long flight to England. Arnie unzips his fleece lined flight suit and stretches it out like a rug, props his B-4 bag behind his back, and opens a can of K-rations.

He speaks into the intercom. "K-ration supply room is now open for business. It ain't filet mignon, but it's better than starving."

Steve crawls out of the tail turret, pulls his bag over and makes himself comfortable. Gus sits alone at the other side of the waist and slowly strokes his gun with an oil rag, staring out over the ocean. He hasn't spoken a word to anyone in hours. Steve points at him and nods. Arnie merely shrugs. They both leave Gus alone with whatever thoughts or demons swirl in his head.

Red and Skeeter sit back on their parachutes, on autopilot. Their eyes scan the full array of instruments every few minutes as an unconscious reflex.

Red calls into the intercom, "Stay alert, everyone. Luftwaffe would love to pick us off if they found us alone out here."

Tex leans over maps on his navigator's desk while Dominick sits in his seat with the fabulous panoramic view from the nose, reading from Ralph Waldo Emerson.

"Listen to this, Tex," he says. "The hero is not fed on sweets, daily his own heart he eats; Chambers of the great are jails, and head winds right for royal sails." He sighs heavily. "That stuff makes you think, doesn't it?"

Tex smiles at his friend. "Yeah, that's good stuff. What would I do without you to educate me?"

"Stay illiterate, I guess."

Dominick gazes out over the water, watching it shimmer endlessly below them. Suddenly he sits up and leans forward. "Hey, what's that?"

Tex hurries over and peers out to where Dominick points. "Looks like a sub. Could it be?"

"Hey, boss," Dominick calls on intercom. "Take a look down there and see if you see what we see."

The German submarine rises higher from the depths and its 20mm cannon opens fire on Betsy as she flies by. Everyone in the plane jumps at the sudden explosion. Number four engine takes a hit, sputters and dies smoking.

Red scrambles to feather the prop and increases power to the other engines. "That son-of-a-bitch! Gunners, we're coming around. Shoot that damn sub right up its ass. Take out that cannon!"

Betsy spins around and dives over the submarine. Gus, Arnie and Steve jump to their guns and make the water boil and ding off the heavy armor. When they hit the cannon, it blows sky high. The whole sub tail seems to be damaged, as it halts and then just floats, dead in the water.

Betsy flies circles around her prey like a vulture.

Red looks out of his window at the floating, quiet sub. "If I had a bomb, I'd drop it on them," he mutters angrily. "Hey Mike, radio headquarters and ask them if they want a trophy. Ask Tex for our position."

"Roger."

Skeeter nervously cranes his head to look all around at the sky. "What if those Germans already radioed the Luftwaffe? We'd be sitting ducks out here alone."

"Hang on. We'll hightail it out of here as soon as they tell us what to do with this tub."

Mike yanks off his earphones with excitement. "Hell yeah, they want it! Orders are to stay put and watch over it. They just scrambled two groups of P-38's with some British Motor Torpedo boats, and a couple of PBY Black Cats from Gibraltar. They're a few minutes away."

"Did you tell them we're on three engines?"

"That's the best part," Mike says gleefully. "We're cordially invited to park at Gibraltar and they'll see to it we have a new engine by tomorrow morning. They've already notified the 44th. Sounds good for us, huh?"

Red smiles, "Well hell, if we don't get shot down in the next few minutes, we'll check out Gibraltar's hospitality, British style. Nice."

Skeeter doesn't look pleased. His eyes continue to dart around the sky. "I just don't like the 'getting shot down' part. They must want that sub pretty bad."

Hal comes onto the flight deck and points out the window. "Here come the P-38's"

The sleek, twin-engine planes streak across the sky at 10,000 feet.

Red takes the flimsy from Mike. "Hey, Little Friends. Big Buddy down here on deck. How does it look?"

A pilot's voice sounds, "The cavalry is on its way. Looks like the Luftwaffe is about to show up, but don't worry. They're our specialty. We'll wait upstairs for them."

The P-38's rise into higher circles.

"There's our protection," Red says and slaps Skeeter's arm. The boy watches apprehensively.

German ME-109's fly in to attack the P-38's, but are badly outnumbered. The Little Friends set on them like wolves to a deer, tearing them apart. A German fighter explodes. Another falls, burning and the pilot ejects and floats to the water in a parachute. The Luftwaffe gives up and leaves.

A fleet of speeding German E-boats races onto the scene, but a formation of PBY Black Cats flies in at 1,000 feet and lays a carpet of bombs over the boats. The P-38's join in the fun and swoop down to open fire on the E-boats and when the spray clears, there is nothing left of them.

The British PT boats arrive and surround the submarine. One boat hooks a tow line to the bow while its sailors usher the German crew out of the sub under machine guns. They load the enemy crew onto the PT's.

Mike hands the radio to Red. The call comes in from a PBY pilot. "B-24, this is Tar Baby. You've been cleared to head to Gibraltar. We'll clean up the rest of this."

"Roger, will do," Red answers. He sends Betsy in the new direction and turns to Skeeter with a British accent. "Onward, mate. Let us hurry to our reception."

Even Skeeter has to grin.

The crew stands outside the huge hanger, duffel bags over their shoulders. Most of them are stripped down to T-shirts with flight suits tied at their waists, except for Gus who wears his suit properly. They contrast dramatically to the British airmen marching by in full uniform, neat and tidy. The grounds of the airbase are equally well groomed, with paved paths and watered lawns.

Red looks around and nods with a satisfied grin. "Well, boys, after Africa, this is lovely."

The hardstands and hangers are full of Lancaster bombers, plywood Mosquitoes, and Spitfires, all lined up smartly along the runways.

A British non-com marches to them and stops, giving them a snappy salute. In his spit-n-polish uniform and with his serious gaunt white face and large nose, he looks as if he were announcing the Queen.

"Lieutenant Rider, sir! Sergeant McGillicuddy, at your service," he practically shouts. "Our commandant, Admiral Shepherd-Moss, requests your presence to welcome you to Gibraltar and to commend you for the extraordinary capture of the German U-boat."

Red grins at him, enjoying the pomp and ceremony. "Lead on, my good man."

"Yessir! This way, sir!" McGillicuddy spins on hard heels and well-polished boots, snaps them together, and stomps away, arms swinging to a measured step. He does not look back at Red and the crew jump to catch up. Red gives a warning glance to each crew member not to imitate their host or joke around. They lift their chins and solemnly follow, trying not to giggle.

Sergeant McGillicuddy swings open the door to an austere, yet elegant office with fine wooden, lacquered furniture and the sense of age and history. Plaques adorn the walls as well as a few glassed frames of antique weapons: guns and swords.

Admiral Shepherd-Moss rises from his seat behind an impressively large desk as Red and the crew enter. He is lean with sharp features, softened only by his genuine smile. The rigid stance of his tall body is natural now after all these years and he looks like a leader accustomed to making tough decisions easily. He steps around his desk to reach Red and shake his hand.

"Congratulations to you and your crew," he says, pumping Red's arm. "I commend you for this achievement."

"Thank you, sir," Red blushes a bit redder, unprepared for the heart-felt warmth from the Admiral.

"You realize that the Allies have never had the opportunity to examine a German U-boat and study its technology. Of course, no one would have guessed a B-24 could capture one," he chuckles at the thought.

"Well, sir, your sea and air crews made it possible."

Admiral leans forward stiffly and taps Red's chest, his smile crinkling the taught skin on his sharp face. "Your crew, Lieutenant, has done a great service to the war effort. That much is true and cannot be denied." He picks up a paper from his desk. "I have been notified that the 8th Air Force Headquarters has already sent a new engine which will arrive tonight. It will take a few days to install. You are welcome to enjoy Gibraltar and I think you'll find it most interesting. Sergeant McGillicuddy will see to your accommodations and help you with anything you need."

He shakes Red's hand again. "Again, congratulations." He moves to each crewman and reverently shakes each hand. The crew salutes him and files out of the office.

Sergeant McGillicuddy leads the crew toward a row of whitewashed barracks, complete with well-tended flowerbeds. He halts and waves a hand at the buildings. "Here we are. Pick any room that suits you in the guest wing then if you would be so kind as to inform the ladies in charge." He consults his watch dramatically. "I will return in precisely one hour to accompany you to dinner."

Arnie can't keep quiet any longer. "Hey, Serg. Maybe Mike and me should hang with you for a while, learn us some good English."

Mike socks him. "Speak for ya'self, Arnie."

McGillicuddy flinches at their hideous accents. He seriously considers the idea for a moment and cracks his first smile with his chest held high. "That would be a splendid proposition. Proper English is the sign of a proper gentleman. Indeed, when I return, we shall begin the lessons."

He snaps a salute and strides away.

Mike punches Arnie again, harder, but his friend only snickers. "Now what'd ya get me into?"

Arnie looks around at the others. "We could all use some refinin', right boys? Make us proper gentlemen. Oh yes!"

Red waves his arms to get attention. "Pick a room, y'all. I'll go talk to the 'ladies'." He bows elegantly and the crew breaks out in catcalls and hoots as he walks to the barrack office.

Red enters the office bustling with maids in immaculate black and white uniforms. They collect towels and cleaning supplies, and they speak softly to each other in Spanish.

He approaches the matron's desk and the woman there turns to him.

His breath catches.

Her smooth olive skin and Spanish almond eyes stimulate a shot of warmth through him. Her voluptuous body gives shape to her matron's dress. Full layers of black hair frame that beautiful face. She smiles brilliantly.

"Lieutenant Rider, I presume." Her Spanish accent sweetly flavors the British words.

"Yes, my lady," he extends a hand to take hers and kisses it regally. Her dark eyes twinkle, amused. The maids step back and giggle.

"You have found rooms to your satisfaction, yes?"

He nods without letting go of her hand. She gently pulls it away.

"I am Teresa Hernandez, your host. Anything you may need would be my pleasure to supply."

He steps closer, his eyes feasting on her shapely frame. "Anything?"

She flushes just a shade, "Your hair, Lieutenant, it is a beautiful color."

"I'm covered with it, all over."

She clears her throat and picks up a clipboard, flustered. "And which rooms will your crew be occupying?"

"I'm not sure," Red frowns as if considering. "I found a problem in my room and was wondering if you'd come have a look at it."

She considers, quickly weighing the risks and the obligations. She glances at the maids who turn away and act as if occupied and not listening to this exchange.

"Alright then," she sighs, sounding official. "We cannot have any problems, now can we? Right, let us have a look."

Arnie sticks his head out of a room and spots Red leading a beautiful woman along the path to the barracks. He whistles. "Hey fellas, look!"

The crewmen pop their heads out to look and their mouths gape.

Red leads Teresa to where Skeeter is standing with his back against the door frame and his eyes wide. Red winks at him. Teresa gives Skeeter and the other boys, who stand there gawking, a luscious smile. Skeeter looks like he will melt into a puddle right there. Red waves her inside. "Please look, I believe there maybe a problem with the bed."

They both step into the perfectly neat cottage with its two beds made with military precision and covered with fluffy beige quilts. Flowers adorn the windows and the little room has a cheery feel to it.

"Could you test the bed for me, please," Red asks in a serious tone that belays his mischievous green eyes. "Perhaps you could push on it to see how it feels to you. My back is extremely tender and the bed has to be soft."

Skeeter slips inside to watch. Teresa's eyes narrow, but she plays along. "Let me see." She leans over the bed, arms straight, and pushes on it. The mattress bounces, as does her cleavage in plain view. Skeeter covers his mouth and backs out, his shoulders shaking.

"The bed feels perfect to me," she concludes. "It should be good for you, and for your back."

Red steps closer and charm oozes from him. "Yes, thank you. I'll walk you back to your office and perhaps you can explain the local entertainment for my crew. We only have a day or two to enjoy your hospitality."

Teresa tries to keep her face blankly official, but this handsome redhead makes her sweat. She touches her tongue to her lips, "Come, I will explain everything to you."

She leads him out of the room and waves demurely at the clustered crew then leads Red back along the path to the office. They all watch her curves move, mesmerized. Red turns to them briefly and smiles. Skeeter rushes into the room, grabs a pillow and bites it.

Red and Teresa stand below the barracks with a group of pretty Spanish maids, now in thin, flowery dresses and heels. Tex, Dominick, Arnie and Steve dash down to meet them, dressed in their finest American fly boy uniforms, hair slicked and face shaved. Tex has even buffed the dust off his Stetson. There are more girls than boys, and some look back at the barracks with exaggerated pouts. Tex and Dominick take two girls each as they walk. Red takes Teresa's hand and waves at those of the crew getting left behind, and the happy group moves off toward town.

Skeeter, Mike, Gus, Hal and Jacob stand near their barrack doors, trying not to look dejected, trying not to look at all. But they are stuck there, staring at the giggling women who are arm-in-arm with their dates. Those lucky men turn and wave, rubbing it in before turning back to their pretty escorts.

"Good thing we're not going," Hal attempts to lift their spirits.

Mike nods, "My mother told me never to mix with the locals." He says it with such finality; he looks around to see if the others believe him.

Skeeter gazes down at his shoes. "Well, I have Suzie and we're engaged. You wouldn't catch me fooling around with Spanish girls. No siree, not me. Sure, she'd never find out, but I'd know, and I wouldn't want to mess up a good thing. We got to go at this marriage right."

Gus slinks into his room and shuts the door.

Hal pokes Jacob. "So why aren't you going? Is it because they aren't Jewish?" Jacob's eyes are glued to the disappearing group. Their laughter reaches them on the sea breeze. He shifts his feet nervously.

Hal pokes him again, trying to get his attention. "You got some Jewish cutie waiting for you back home? Gonna settle down with her when this is over? Or is it that your mama told you never to look at a girl less she's Jewish?"

Jacob glances at Hal with a flash of sudden panic. "Um, see ya later." And he dashes after the group, calling and waving to them.

"Damn traitor," Mike growls. The forlorn boys stand there like abandoned orphans.

"Oh hell," Skeeter says, "McGillicuddy said they're showing a movie at the mess hall. Let's go."

The three shuffle down the path, heads bowed.

"I bet they get some," Mike mumbles.

"Yeah, some disease!" Hal admonishes.

Skeeter blows out a huge sigh. "Oh shut up already!" They trudge on like whipped puppies.

Three days later, Red steps out of the barrack office and smiles smugly. He wipes lipstick off his mouth with a handkerchief.

Sergeant McGillicuddy clears his throat and startles him. "Excuse me, sir!"

"Yes, Sergeant."

"The 8th Air Force has called to reroute your travel plans, sir. Orders are for all bomber groups to head for Tunis, North Africa."

Red's jaw drops. "Oh God, no."

Sympathy softens the Sergeant's face. "I quite understand your feelings, sir. Extremely disappointing not to be stationed in England." He shakes his head dramatically. "Such is the nature of war, if I may say so."

"Damn."

Sergeant ventures a hand on Red's shoulder, commiserating. "Truly a tragedy, sir. I have been informed that American troops are detained at the beachhead on the coast of Italy and haven't been able to break through. Your bombers are to soften their position."

Red rubs a hand over his face. Images of sand, hot sun and ugly Arabs flash before his eyes.

"They are giving you four days to get there. If you leave tomorrow you could sojourn at Algiers for a respite. I've heard it is a wonderful city. They have a very entertaining night life, thanks to the Free French Resistance Fighters."

Red looks up and smiles. "What would we do without you and your wonderful wealth of knowledge?" He grabs McGillicuddy's hand and pumps it emphatically. "Indeed, it has been a great pleasure to receive your hospitality. We'll never forget you, Sergeant. Thank you!"

McGillicuddy sputters, loses decorum momentarily as he is deeply pleased by the praise. Quickly he remembers himself and snaps to a rigid salute, his face glowing.

"The feeling is mutual, sir!" he barks and strides away as if late for the parade. Red chuckles and heads for the barracks to tell the boys the good and bad news.

6

Betsy floats from the sea and looms larger and larger as she approaches a Mediterranean harbor filled with fishing boats and white sails. Algiers is an ancient, whitewashed jewel splashed up an eight hundred foot hillside above the harbor. Halfway up, the Casbah's fortified walls impose themselves over the town.

Betsy descends like a majestic swan to the airfield beyond the city on the ocean bluff.

The duffel-laden crew walks toward the Operations building off the runway. It's a newer building, hastily thrown up like a tin can to serve the war effort.

"First on the agenda," Red announces to his charges. "We drop our stuff and go explore this town."

Tex grins, "I'm getting a hang of this night life scene."

Dominick slaps him on the back. "What was her name? Juanita? She had you converted, huh?"

Tex raises his hands in acquiesce. "I confess. That little Spanish gal had me singin' serenades."

Hal and Mike huff and snort, not wanting to hear anything about the Spanish dates. Steve raises his hand as if in class. "I read about the Casbah. It's like a fort, but also an Arab palace. Hell, I bet it's complete with a harem." He smacks Arnie. "Hey, that would make a great name for your whorehouse! Only problem is, nobody in Brooklyn would know what it meant."

"He should just be straight forward about it and call it 'whorehouse'," Mike says. "It's Brooklyn after all. What do you expect?"

"Or call it 'Jerkoff's'," Hal adds. "Since he won't find enough girls to run a full fledged business."

Meanwhile, Arnie is paying no heed to any of their bantering. He is busy shuffling through scraps of paper from his wallet. He finds what he's looking for and holds it up for Red to see. "Would you believe I got my aunt's address here in Algiers? Guys look! She's my aunt, my dad's sister, and I haven't even met her before! Dad wrote this down for me in case I got this far. And here we are! What do ya think, boss? Think I should check it out?"

Red stops and peers at the worn piece of paper. "That's fantastic, Arnie! You actually have family here. Now's a perfect time to meet her."

They all gather around Arnie and his scrap of paper. "My dad left in the '20's to make something of himself in New York," he tells them. "Met my mom and never came back here. He didn't even tell me about his family until I was leaving for Europe. Then he gave me this, said if I get near Algiers I should look her up."

He looks around at them and suddenly he's a nineteen-year-old needing reassurance. "Think she'd even want to see me?"

Hal nods enthusiastically. "Hell, yes! Of course she would! You're the nephew she never got to meet!"

"He's right," Dominick adds. "For sure she'll love meeting you."

Skeeter touches Arnie's arm. "You have got to try. She may miss your father and get a real kick out of seeing you."

"Then it's settled," Red says. "First on the agenda is finding Arnie's family."

They all pat Arnie as they walk on to the Operations building.

The crew wonders through narrow, winding streets buzzing with life. The afternoon sea breeze wafts through the streets and cools off the town as sunlight reflects off of the white-washed walls. Venders crowd every corner, enticing last minute shoppers to buy. The populous teems with all nations and races, some dressed in European garb, some in traditional Arab dress, and some women are covered in long veils. The cooling breeze smells of ocean and gently rustles the vine flowers dangling off of white balconies.

The crew stops as Arnie asks anyone who looks like they speak English, and shows his piece of paper. Some shrug and walk away. One old man points up a street and indicates a turn. The crew follows Arnie as he ascends the street, turns onto another, smaller street and searches for house numbers. He sees a blue door with the name Weiss in black letters. His buddies stay on the street and wait as he slowly approaches the door.

Now Arnie stands alone in front of it. He hesitates.

"Nothin' to lose for tryin'" Tex encourages him. Arnie grins back at them nervously. He knocks.

After a moment, a young man opens the door. His eyes open wide. About the same age as Arnie, the two look strikingly alike, as if twins. They stare at each other for a bazaar moment.

"This the Weiss residence?" Arnie chokes on the words.

"Yes. You are American?"

"I'm Arnold Weiss from Brooklyn, New York. I'm looking for my father's family. You look like the right Weiss."

A broad grin spreads over the cousin's face. He grabs Arnie in a bear hug and kisses his cheeks.

"Whoa there!" Arnie sputters. "Hang on!" But the cousin is shouting into the house.

"Mama! Mama! Your brother from America! His son is here! Come quick!"

Mama appears, shoving cousin aside as she dries her hands on her apron. She's in her forties with a matronly body and a face that has worried often, and her resemblance to Arnie's father is unmistakable. She stares between the two boys and her dark eyes swim with tears to see how much they look alike.

Her arms shoot out and she buries Arnie in her embrace. "My nephew! I cannot believe it!"

She kisses him profusely before allowing him to step back and catch his breath. She points to his uniform. "What is this?

You are soldier?"

Arnie is flushed and wobbly, and he points at his grinning crew. "American Air Force, Auntie. We fly!"

She steps out onto the street without letting go of Arnie's hand and smiles at the crew as tears trickle down her round cheeks. "This is great day for us. My brother is gone so long. You bring my nephew. Thank you. God bless you for this gift."

Red steps forward. "Our pleasure, ma'am."

Mama wipes her eyes with her multipurpose apron and nods at Red's hair. "Beautiful color. You must have many girlfriends."

"He sure does," Skeeter answers for him.

Mama pulls Arnie back to the doorway. "You all come in. I make cake and tea, plenty for everyone."

"We're just here for tonight, Auntie. Got to leave tomorrow," Arnie says. His cousin puts an affectionate hand on his back.

"You must stay with us tonight," he says. "Then you come back again as soon as you can."

"Yes," Mama agrees. "You stay here. This is your home."

"Wow, thanks," Arnie is at a loss for words.

Red says, "You can stay if you want to, Arnie."

The boy looks at him, then at his cousin and aunt who flank him. He smiles. "Yeah, I do."

"Ok then," Red agrees. "You can take the bus back to the base tomorrow. Flight time is 3 o'clock. So stay and enjoy yourself."

Mama takes charge and corrals them all.

"First you eat!" she insists. She encircles Arnie's waist and takes her own son's arm, and with renewed tears flowing, she leads them all inside.

The Palace Theater is an old-style nightclub with a center stage and smoky tables all around. The crew takes up two tables close to the stage and sip beer. The other tables fill up quickly with mostly French men and women in evening suits and gowns, sipping cocktails. The crew is conspicuous in American uniforms as they look around and drink from their bottles. The French patrons smile and nod to them. They are all Allies.

The house lights dim. The stage brightens on a single microphone.

Hush through the room.

The MC's voice resounds, "Mademoiselle Yvette Leleu."

The audience is utterly silent as a woman steps into the light. She is dazzlingly beautiful. At twenty-two, her slim body glistens in the black, full-length gown. Her black hair accentuates ivory skin. But it's her eyes that speak. Dark and bright, they gaze out over the packed room, and pause on Red. Her full lips part in a smile.

Music emanates from the piano.

She sings a French melody of love in a rich mezzo soprano. The notes pour from her and mesmerize the crowd.

Red gapes at her and feels the meaning of the words she sings, captivated to the point where he completely loses all sense of the passage of time. At first she sings to everyone in the room, but then she catches Red's stare and their eyes lock. After several songs, she pulls the mic stand to the edge of the stage and sings to him alone.

Red's face flushes, and he stiffens in his seat. It seems they are totally alone as this Goddess pours out her heart to him.

She stops and a sudden roar rises from the crowd. She bows and waves to all. As she backs away, their voices cheer in unison for more. She walks back to the mic and after the room quiets she begins to sing the French National Anthem, "La Marseillaise."

Chairs scrape and the entire room gets to their feet. Red and the crew jump to attention. The walls reverberate with one great voice.

The crew engages in a beer-soaked conversation, creating a little island of English amid the mass of French chatter around them. Red sits back from the table and watches the back stage door. His whole being is on edge, waiting, anticipating Yvette's arrival. He knows with a certainty she will come.

There she is, slipping out of the door and weaving her way among the tables. The pale of her skin is like the finest quality porcelain against the black velvet of her lush hair. She shakes hands with many of the appreciative patrons and pauses to exchange a word.

Red gets up and walks to her, moving to stand before her and block out all others. She radiates a smile, her dark eyes flashing, and reaches for his hand. Their hands embrace and both of their faces flush with shock at what they feel.

Yvette recovers first. "What's your name, soldier?" She speaks with a perfect American accent.

For the first time in his life Red stutters. "I'm a…. my name is…" He stops. They stand very close. He catches her scent of some delicious perfume. "Uh, I'm Red Rider, Air Force pilot."

"I can see why they call you Red."

"Are you really French or an American in disguise?"

Yvette chuckles, those lips parting and her eyes dancing, "Disguise I know well, but this is not one. I am quite French, Monsieur Red. And proud of it."

Their bodies almost touch. Electric fields of heat light up between them. He stares deeply into the darkness of her eyes, and feels the warmth from her bare arms and porcelain neck. They stand there as if alone.

"I've never heard a more melodic voice," Red says quietly.

"It was my profession before the war."

"Was?"

He sees a sudden pain wash across her face, a sorrow of great trials played out just under the surface.

"We all have a new career now, to free the world of tyranny," she says.

He takes her hand again in both of his and boldly intertwines his fingers in hers. He cannot let this moment escape. "War changes everything," he pauses, connecting with her. "It even changes how a man meets the love of his life and there's no time to hide it or play games."

Yvette's face grows serious. She whispers, "You pressure much, Red Rider." But she does not pull away. Instead, she closes the tiny gap between them. Red's heart races.

He whispers, "Perhaps we can retire somewhere more private and discuss this."

"I never take men home." Her full lips are so close, parted over white teeth.

"You were waiting for me," Red insists.

Dominick taps Red on the shoulder and backs away when Red's flushed face turns on him. "We were hoping you'd introduce us," he says defensively. He slinks back to the others who wait there at the tables in eager anticipation. They all stand respectfully.

"Yeah, share the wealth, Lieutenant," Tex drawls.

Swallowing the interrupted moment, Red turns Yvette to them. She nods as they bow. "Meet my crew. The crème of the Air Force. Copilot Skeeter, Bombardier Dominick, Navigator Tex, who thankfully left his Stetson behind. That's engineer Hal. Radioman Mike and Tail Gunner Steve both need lessons in English. Tunnel Gunner Jacob the Nazi Killer, and hiding behind him there is Waist Gunner Gus."

"It is a great pleasure to meet you," she says. "May I speak for the French people and thank you for risking your lives to free Europe. Everyone of you is so important to the war effort."

The crew stammers with blushes. Skeeter says, "You speak English like us. Well, I mean better than us."

"I went to high school and college in Boston. Graduated from the New England Conservatory of Music," she explains.

"You really have a lovely voice, ma'am," Tex says, making a gesture to tip his hat, forgetting he's not wearing it.

"How'd ya get from Boston to Algiers?" Steve asks. Red cuts in and steers her away from the tables.

"Yes, well, I know you have lots of questions, boys. But Miss Leleu has very important information to debrief me on concerning the Free French. So say good-night now to the lady."

His eyes shut their mouths. Yvette smiles and allows him to guide her out. The crew mumbles their good-nights as the couple disappears.

"How does he do that?" Skeeter mumbles in wonder.

"Damn, I wish I knew," Dominick says.

Tex gathers them together and heads them for the door. "Crazy Red's got more than the red hair goin' for him, that's for sure."

Yvette's apartment is one tiny room with moonlight entering through thin curtains from the balcony window. A miniature kitchenette takes up a corner, a neatly made bed in another with a table, two chairs and a free-standing armoire. A door leads to the bathroom.

Yvette lights a candle on the table and its soft glow warms the moonlight.

"Do you live alone here?" Red asks.

"Of course."

"How can that be? A woman as gorgeous and talented as you must have thousands of men clamoring for you."

She turns to him with a look that he will soon come to recognize: a face hardened by trials, frank and honest. "He's dead. My husband was killed a year ago in Paris when the Gestapo took every newspaper writer and shot them in public."

She moves away for a moment and opens the window to the night breeze and the full light. Red's arms encircle her gently from behind.

"I'm sorry," he says in her hair.

She remains silent and he holds her for a very long moment.

"You said you never bring men home. Why am I here?"

He turns her to him and entwines his fingers in her hand. His other hand caresses the hair from her face. Her black eyes shine large and silver in the moonlight.

"Why do you ask?"

His face is serious. "I just want us both to know what this

is not."

"When I touched you – "

"I knew."

He lifts the gown over her head and steps back, enjoying the almost nakedness of her. "Oh, my lady," he groans. He watches her as if time has stopped and she stands before him with radiant milky skin. He unbuttons his shirt, slips out of pants, and drops them to the side. He moves to kiss her face and neck, his hands touching everywhere with light caresses. She arches to him and he lays her on the bed. His lips travel softly over her.

Quietly she moans. He kisses her harder.

The crew waits in front of the plane, unwilling to board and miss the scene. Arnie hugs and kisses his aunt and cousin. He picks up the heavy basket of goodies she has lovingly packed for him, and he waves, joining the others.

Red lingers in an embrace, gazing into Yvette's eyes. "I'm coming back. Tunis is only two hours away. I'll be here."

Her sigh shakes her whole body. "I'll wait for you."

"And when we get sent to England, I'm taking you with me. I'll figure out a way." He kisses her long and slowly, and whispers in her ear, "We're going to beat this war, you'll see."

She pulls back and looks at him. "Our lives are not in our hands. War makes all of the decisions. We have to accept our small part in it."

Red shakes his head adamantly, "No. We're going to survive and be together. I'll make it happen." He grips her hard, "This war will end. Life will go on and it'll be worth living."

But the look of somber resignation in her face frightens him. He knows it is born of the great losses she has suffered, and his words are just words from someone whose country has never been attacked on native soil. Can a person suffer too much and not recover?

Yvette pushes him toward the crew. "Au revoir, amour." Red shoos the crew in through the bomb bay doors then turns and waves. Yvette moves to where Arnie's family stands on the tarmac. Mama gazes knowingly at her.

"Beautiful hair on that man, eh?"

Yvette watches the propellers whir to life and the plane taxi away with Red and Arnie waving out the windows. "Yes, a beautiful man."

Yvette links arms with Mama and together they walk slowly from the runway. In war, all you can do is pray, never knowing if your paths will ever cross again. The two women give strength to each other.

7

Betsy lowers toward a bulldozed strip of sand, with olive-drab tents strung along the low hills around and a few B-24's parked to the side. There is a beat-up, wooden control tower that looks like a tall outhouse.

Red lands her on the runway and kicks up enough dust for a solar eclipse. He calls to the crew over the intercom. "Cover your guns, boys. Keep that sand out. We're home sweet home."

Skeeter scoffs, "All we need to see is a couple of Arabs on camels."

"Don't remind me."

Steve's voice coughs on the intercom. "You're killing me back here!Can't breathe!"

They roll to a stop, lined up with the other battle-weary planes and wait for a moment for the dust to settle. Then they crawl out of the plane and Bob greets them with a wide, gaping grin and a muscular handshake.

Red grins back at him. "You're like a flea I can't get rid of. Everywhere we go, you're there ahead of us."

"I try to be, but you keep getting sidetracked. I hear you have the most fun around here," Bob nudges him and winks.

Lowel and Whitie join them, looking like opposites. Lowel is stripped to his sweaty black chest, while Whitie wears his coverall zipped up, complete with a Jacob-style rag over his head and neck.

"How's the new engine?" Whitie asks.

"Just give her gas and she goes," Red says.

Bob chuckles, "Like some girls I know."

Red lifts his eyebrows at him. "Really? And you *know* them?"

Skeeter gets between them. "So what's Tunis like?"

Whitie swings his arm around. “What you see is what you get. Desert’s asshole, worse than Benghazi, so go set yourselves up at the Ritz tents.” He points to the tent-dotted hills.

Bob gets serious. “So this is the deal. They don’t need you guys in Italy anymore, so day after tomorrow there’s a big mission into Europe. We’re supposed to equip you with extra fuel and heavy bombs.”

The crew goes silent as their faces sink. Bob realizes what he’s done to their mood, too late. “Anyway, they’ll tell you about it at the briefing. We’ll get to work on Betsy. See you guys back here this afternoon.”

The crew moves as a pack grudgingly toward the hills. Steve grumbles, “Remind me why I signed up for this.” Nobody comments.

Tent city at night looks more like an Indian camp except for the pale-face men. The crews all gather around a bonfire crackling in the center. Tex stands guard over it, being his creation. Satisfied, he pulls the Stetson low over his eyes and sits to watch and think. But as more and more men arrive, and a few bottles get passed around, the mood switches from meditative to festive. More than a hundred men chat and laugh and get increasingly drunk.

Somebody pulls a crank-arm phonograph out of a tent and strains of melodious music float over the desert.

Red sits next to Skeeter and watches the scene. A couple of Irishmen start dancing a fancy jig and all hell breaks loose as others join in and make it like a competition. Even Tex gets up and starts Texan foot stomping wildly around his fire, yipping like a coyote. Sand kicks up everywhere.

Red sighs, not in the mood. “Think I’ll go over to the Officer’s Club.”

“Want company?” Skeeter asks, not being the dancing type. Red puts his arm around his copilot’s shoulders and squeezes.

“I can’t think of anyone I’d rather hang around with than

you, Skeeter. But tonight I need to be alone for a while."

Skeeter peers at him, not offended. He nods. "Yvette's on your mind."

"And in my heart," Red sighs again. He pats his friend's back and slips away in the darkness.

Red enters the make-shift building that doubles as a Red Cross outpost. The room is filled with quiet conversations as officers sit at card tables and sip drinks and eat what looks incredibly like bowls of ice cream. Red heads for the bar and sits. He notices a grand piano in the corner, lusciously polished as if it belonged in Carnegie Hall. What a strange sight it is, to come in from a barren desert in this God-forsaken land and find a concert piano.

A woman dressed as a Red Cross nurse, with prim white cap and all, is bar tending. They must think a bit of alcohol is medicinal. She gives him a friendly, homey smile, sweet and blond, as if she were a poster girl for American farms.

"Can I get you some ice cream?" she says those magical words.

"You've got to be kidding!"

She giggles, showing a dimple. "I kid you not. Homemade and fresh, we make is everyday and serve it every afternoon here. Today's vanilla!"

Red acts as if in the throws of ecstasy. "Say no more. Serve me up some, please."

She scoops out a heaping bowlful from a freezer box behind the bar, and slides it to him. "Enjoy!"

Red takes a bite and closes his eyes with pleasure. "Thank you, ma'am!"

She watches him savor it, as pleased as a mother for her child. Red Cross nurses see precious little happiness, especially in this war-torn desert. If a bowl of ice cream can help a fly boy feel a taste of home, it lightens her heart.

Red doesn't notice the room go quiet, until the nurse hurries around the bar.

"He's here!" she says.

She rushes to the grand piano and lifts its top and props it open. A gaunt old man has shuffled into the room and as he leans on his cane, he scans the now silent room with bright eyes and totters feebly to the piano. He is dressed in an old and well-worn, yet neat gentleman's dark suit, a scarlet silk scarf tucked artistically in his collar. He sinks with a groan to the bench and lays down his cane. The nurse hurries back to the bar and watches eagerly. A sense of anticipation fills the room.

"What's going on?" Red whispers to her. The nurse simply nods toward the old man as he raises his fingers to the keys and his bent back straightens. He begins to play and suddenly the room is filled with Beethoven. Red stares in disbelief. He watches the cords of muscle work in the old hands as the composition is played to perfection.

The nurse leans across the bar and whispers to Red, "Before the war, he was a famous concert pianist in Germany. When Hitler started rounding up the Jews, he went underground. He resurfaced here, of all places, in North Africa. They say he was trying to get to Palestine and gave up." She lowers her voice even more, her face soft with compassion for the old gentleman. "He's got no one left. We give him food and a little place to live. He gives us beautiful music every afternoon."

Red nods, "Sad story."

She shrugs, her smile falters as she resumes cleaning behind the bar. "The world is full of sad stories these days."

Red hands her the empty bowl. "Well, thank you. Never knew ice cream could taste so good." He sits for another moment, listening to the melodies floating from the piano. "Damn crazy war. Nothing but destruction of all the beauty of life. Nothing will ever be the same."

Nurse leans toward him and admonishes with a finger. "Don't get attached to anyone. That's my advice. Don't let yourself be vulnerable."

Red rears back. She doesn't seem to notice the effect of her words on him as she busies herself cleaning. But he feels the weight of her words like a premonition. Yvette's face flashes before his eyes. Shaken, he tries to regain his control. "Sell me a bottle of brandy, please."

"Tunisian?" she asks. "Nasty stuff. It'll blow your head off."

"I'm tough."

She hands him a bottle and takes his money, watching him tuck it in his shirt.

"Thank you, ma'am, for a memorable evening."

She sighs mightily. "Yeah, I wish they all said that!"

Red passes the piano and nods to the masterful pianist and displaced genius, and leaves.

Red sits on a bench in a clapboard briefing hut packed with pilots and crews, all staring with apprehensive silence at the wall map where Colonel Jensen points. A string runs from Tunis, across the Mediterranean, over Italy and Austria to a point near Vienna.

"Weiner Neustadt," Jensen is saying. "The Messerschmitt factory. It's high priority and heavily fortified."

The Colonel's voice fades as Red's guts pull tight. "Heavily fortified" rings in his ears. Jensen is reading instructions for navigators, radio men, and bombardiers. Red momentarily tunes out. Yvette's face appears with the surprised expression during those first moments when they had touched. She smiles and brings her red lips to his.

Colonel Jensen snaps him back. "Good luck, boys. God be with us all." He steps down and the Chaplain moves to the front. He is not as young as the Chaplain at Benghazi, but he looks just as haggard. He gazes over the full room, and the pain of knowing is evident in his eyes. "Let's bow our heads in prayer." They all obey.

The squadrons fly in tight formation five miles above the sea. Every angle exposes a gun and every crew member looks sharp. Betsy flies tail-end-Charlie of the high squadron with a sweeping view of all other ships.

On the flight deck, Mike listens intently to the radio headphones pressed into his ears. Hal finishes equipment and gauge checks and quietly disappears into the top turret. There is no conversation as each man waits, wonders and fears.

Mike pulls the headphones off and sits back, looking deeply worried. "Lieutenant, I turned on the German frequency." Red glances back at him and sees his pallor. "They're yelling nothing but 'Actung Luftwaffe'!" He stares at Red with haunted eyes. "Do you suppose that means..."

"They're waiting for us. Yeah, I'd guess that's right. Damn spies work fast."

Skeeter wipes his dry lips with a trembling hand.

The formation of mighty birds flies straight for the Italian coast line, and out of the mist three German FW-190's rise like a cobra and line up to strike. It's a head-on collision as they zip into the formation, 20mm canons flashing fire from their wings. B-24 gunners answer with blinding fire power.

Two FW-190's explode. The other peels off. A B-24 in the low squadron bursts into flames. Parachutes blossom and spiral down as the formation tightens.

On the flight deck, Red feels every one of his senses sharpen, focused on controlling the big bird in formation. As he plays this game of tag with death, the metallic smell of adrenaline fills him.

Skeeter watches out the window as the parachutes disappear. "I hope they're good swimmers," he mutters.

Red checks the sky around them. "Heavy stuff already. They're coming, I can feel them."

Skeeter grips his wheel and blanches. "Keep us in the air, boss. You've got to keep us up."

Dominick's voice comes over the intercom. "Fighters at 11 o'clock high. Fighters at 6 o'clock."

"Here they come," Red says.

Luftwaffe appear from everywhere at once and dive bonsai-style at the formation. Weighted with fuel and bombs, the B-24's blow up as Luftwaffe bullets tear into them. Gunners blast the quick F-190's as they dart in and out, and soon the sky is filled with falling fire balls. The formation disintegrates as planes avoid hitting debris. The lumbering armada moves inexorably into Austria.

A brace of ME-109's streaks through the squadron. The ship in front of Betsy bursts into flames and wheels away.

Red pushes forward to tack onto the next ship. He tries to clear his mind of everything but survival. Fly this ship. Dodge the deadly dangers. Keep them alive.

He holds tight to the steering, leaning slightly forward and feels the plane moving as if an extension of his body, evasive like a boxer. Adrenaline pumps through his veins, pounds in his ears as if he were charged with electricity.

Outside the window they watch in horror as an airman tucked in a ball spins by the wing with no parachute and is gone. The smoky, acrid smell of burnt cordite drifts through the plane as the guns vibrate the ship. Each man concentrates on his job, doing his part to stay alive.

Suddenly a 20mm canon shell tears into the cockpit and blow up between them. Red is deafened and blinded by the bang and the flash for precious seconds as he tries to keep control of the plane and steady her. When his vision clears he sees blood everywhere, hanging from the instruments in dripping tendrils, and the wind is sucking through the hole in the cockpit wall. His ears ring dully and his eyes are blurred, but he turns to look at Skeeter and recoils violently. Headless, the copilot slumps in his chair, the blood that has gushed out of the stump of his body and sprayed all over the controls is slowing down and now dribbles over his flight suit to the floor.

Red's stomach shoves into his throat, his breath choked off as it he were strangled.

"Mike," he shrieks. "Get Skeeter!"

No choice but to keep flying, he fights the paralysis of wrenching pain to keep the plane moving through the gauntlet of debris and killer Luftwaffe. He can't look anywhere but forward, and he struggles to keep the blood out of his eyes and his vision clear.

Mike must have been knocked off the flight deck by the blast. He now dashes back and tries to stop short, but slips and falls in the pooled blood with an anguished cry. "Oh my God! Skeeter!" Red can hear his shallow, panic breathing, the sound of stifled gagging. "Blood! So much!"

"Get him out of there," Red barks without looking. Mike grabs Skeeter's body, unleashes him from the seat and lowers him to the deck.

"Skeeter, no, God, no," Mike stands back staring, frozen. Red swings out his arm and smacks Mike on the back, enough to wake him up.

"Get a rag and wipe off the instruments. I can't see anything."

Mike points at Red, horror twisting his face. "You! You're covered in it. Your face!"

Red touches the burn cutting across his cheek. He feels the sting and wet of Skeeter's blood in it. "Never mind me," he says. "Go do what I asked." He wipes his eyes as blood threaten to work into the sweat washing over his face. Mike disappears.

Tex's voice blasts from the intercom. "Navigator to pilot. We're crossing into Austria, about an hour from target."

Red gulps on his own sorrow. No one else knows what happened to Skeeter. He can't think about their reactions now. *Another hour of this? May as well be 10 years.*

Mike returns with a rag and gingerly tries to wipe the controls. He is pale and shaking and looks like he already vomited back in the hold. "It's a mess," he mutters, tears in his eyes. "I can't get it off."

Red grabs his arm. "Go back to your station."

Mike stares at the bloody rag in his hand and at the body stretched out on the floor. "Skeeter..."

"I know. Leave him now. Go do your job. We've got a long way to go."

Mike nods and drops the rag, hurries away.

Alone, Red turns back to the battle at hand, clearing his mind of all thoughts, letting instinct take over.

In the sky over Austria the air war rages on. Like a flock of great geese attacked by many small vicious black birds, B-24's explode as Luftwaffe jet through their formation. They too blow up and dive, screaming and spiraling down to their death. Colored German parachutes mingle with white American parachutes of those lucky enough to get out. Those battle-weary little birds retreat to refuel, as fresh Luftwaffe fly onto the scene to take up the assault.

Two planes in Betsy's squadron take hits. One loses 3 engines and the parachuting crew leaps out. The other bursts into flames and 3 men jump out on fire, parachutes burning. They drop fast.

The squadron of twelve is now reduced to four planes. The whole formation is a third of its original size. Betsy looks like a flying sieve, full of holes.

On the flight deck, Red is more alone than ever in his life, flying her with white knuckles, maneuvering her through the sky because he is the only one who can. He watches helplessly as another wave of ME-109's zips through the planes, belching out hot lead and canon shells. Times like this, he wishes he had his own gun and not the control over the lives of every other man on this ship.

In Betsy's tail, Steve swivels in his tiny seat, shooting left and right, catching Luftwaffe and strafing their bellies.

Jacob locks onto a passing F-190 and sends it smoking to earth.

Gus shoots with cool accuracy.

Arnie mutters curses as he slams more ammunition in his gun and fires. Every man works his position, fighting to shoot and kill before they are shot.

Tex glances at the calculations on his desk and hurries to help man the guns with Dominick in the nose. Non of them are aware of their dead comrade up on the flight deck. They focus on the task at hand.

"Half an hour away. I don't see us keeping up with this onslaught," Tex says. Dominick shoots at a passing Luftwaffe as it streaks by. They are watching the action from ring side seats, watching the sky boil with debris, not stopping to wonder when something might smash through the glass nose and kill them.

"Onslaught?" Dominick comments. "Did I teach you that word?"

Tex points to their reduced squadron flying high and leading the others. "We're sitting ducks out here." They both shoot as Luftwaffe descend on them.

In the top turret, Hal sees them coming, his position vulnerable, like a bulb sticking out of the top of Betsy. A whole flock of fire-spitting planes descends upon her. He focuses on one and shoots. As if in slow motion, he sees the canon shell zooming straight for him. In less than a second he knows it will hit. Hal simply closes his eyes, and his hands release his gun. BOOM!

Red feels the plane shake on impact. With a fresh shudder of sickness he knows. "Mike! Top turret!" he shouts. He hears Mike move to the ladder, but he can't turn away from guiding the plane through the opposition. Strangled sobs reach his dulled ears. Moments pass. Nothing but the rumble of explosions outside send shock waves through Betsy's damaged skin.

Mike's voice reaches across the bloody flight deck, choking in falsetto. "He's gone. Hal's gone. Nothing's left of him."

Red doesn't respond. Nausea blurs his vision. He presses the oxygen to his mouth and forces himself to breathe deeply. Forces himself to push away the crushing darkness. Looking straight ahead, he sees an entire squadron of ME-109's line up to attack. Sudden anger rushes through him, a powerful, adrenaline-pumping sensation, crawling up his spine and feeding his muscles new force.

"Pilot to crew," he calls in to the intercom. "From now on,

if you see a fighter come in range, say 'go'."

The ME-109's swarm in like hornets. Dominick's voice shouts, "Go!"

Betsy suddenly drops out of tail-end-Charlie position and does a gyrating dance of bobbing and weaving as if in the throws of death. ME-109's zero in on the other planes and give the crazed B-24 a wide berth. Their pilots must fear her exploding and sending debris all over them. They shoot at the other big birds instead.

Red pulls Betsy back up and sees the holes in three other planes ahead of him. No guilt, he focuses only on the survival of this plane and the rest of his crew.

"They're coming back," Steve informs from the tail. "Go!"

Betsy rolls down and shakes, seemingly out of control. The Luftwaffe pass over her and blast the last three planes left in the squadron. One explodes in a flash of fire. Another loses three engines and dives to earth. The last loses vertical fins and the left wing and spins, screaming down.

Betsy flies solo. She swoops down to the only squadron left and tacks onto the back.

The flight deck looks like a scene from a horror movie. Drying blood dangles from the controls and the seats. Splatters hang from the ceiling. Wind roars through the holes in the walls. The headless body drains in a huge puddle that spreads over the whole deck. How can one body hold so much blood?

But Red can't think about that. He breathes through his mouth, trying not to become overwhelmed by the foul coppery smell mingling with gunpowder. He sits alone like some macabre figure, drenched in blood. Only his eyes glow with seething anger and stare ahead toward whatever comes next.

"Two minutes from the IP," Tex announces.

"Roger," Red answers. "Ready, Dom?"

"Roger," Dominick calls back. He must hear something different in Red's voice. "You ok, boss?"

"Just make this worth it. Some how."

Dominick pauses a second, glances at Tex and shrugs. He

says into the intercom, "We'll clobber them, boss. I promise. Opening bomb bay doors."

As if they have seen a ghost, the Luftwaffe disappear. The struggling formation of B-24's follow their leader and open up over the IP.

Suddenly a new killer attacks. Flak explodes like black blossoms of death and pepper the air all around them. One bursts close to Betsy and sprays her flank with new holes, forcing her to bounce like a toy. Ahead of her, a ship takes a direct hit and the vicious shards of metal rip her wing off. She waffles toward earth, breaking up and scattering debris all the way down.

The lead ship drops her load and all others follow suit.

In the tail turret, Steve leans forward and watches the bombs drop on the massive factory, laying out a blanket of fire and destruction. "We smashed them!" he calls on the intercom.

Betsy follows the others on the turn, out of the flak area, and heads southeast. Steve spots an F-190 sneaking up on them. "Fighter at five o'clock high! Go!"

Betsy dives into her wounded-bird act and Steve shoots with a fury. "Die, sucker!" he growls. "Got him!"

The F-190 shatters into a million pieces.

The ragged bomber group drones steadily toward the Mediterranean over Italy. Some cough on two engines and putter precariously in the air. Others are missing partial wings, tails or turrets, and all have holes big enough to walk through.

A fleet of Italian fighter planes swarms in circles just out of firing range. Dominick and Tex watch the Italians as they make no moves to advance.

"What, are they sightseeing?" Dominick asks. "Never seen a bunch of banged up B-24 before?"

Tex snorts. "Chicken shit. They know better than to engage us. We can still blast their asses off."

"Let 'em try it."

Tex nudges his companion and points to the sea ahead.

They can make out the line of desolate desert beyond. "Home sweet home."

"Do you think we'll make it? Boss must be dead tired."

Tex squeezes his shoulder and turns back to his navigation desk. "He's tough. We'll make it." Neither one of them wants to say what they are thinking. They don't want to know yet who may have been killed or injured. They just know that the ship did not get through this one unscathed. There will be time enough to find out, and then to try to survive more missions with more horrific air battles. Better not to think at all, for now.

The formation heads for Tunis runway. Several planes with shot-out hydraulics turn toward the desert sand. They fly in slow, unable to lower landing gear, and belly flop, skidding along, raising huge waves of dust and sand.

Red leans over Skeeter's switches and manages to flip down the landing gear and adjust the flaps while holding the steering wheel with one hand and the throttle with his knees. He sits down in time to land Betsy smoothly on the runway and taxi to the hardstand and stop. He switches everything off and the sudden and complete silence slams down on him and sinks him into his chair. He folds his arms over the control column, leans over and buries his head. Dried blood makes a tight mask over his face and hands, though his burned cheek has gone too numb to feel. Tremors run down his back and he is barely breathing. For a moment it seems as if he will pass out. He can feel his conscious wavering, a deeper blackness to fall into behind the black of his closed eyes.

Tex and Dominick rush onto the deck and stop short, staring a the horrible scene, stepping where their boots are already in blood. They see Skeeter's headless corpse and shudder.

Tex calls to the blood-covered man hunched over the controls. "Boss?" No response. "Can we help you, boss?"

After a long moment they wonder if he has passed out. But then they hear a muffled "No."

Tex and Dominick exchange a look then turn away. Red needs a moment and they need to stop looking at the body of their friend. They squeeze by the top turret ladder and see blood puddled on the deck below with shreds of flesh hanging from every rung. They choke down the bile and move back through the plane, gathering what's left of the crew, informing them of the casualties. They find Mike leaning over his radio is a complete daze.

Bob, Whitie and Lowel look around the hardstands in shock. The crew staggers out of the damaged ship, sweaty and smoke-stained, blood on their boots. Wearily they yank off flight suits and gear, regardless of the burning afternoon sun.

Bob steps forward. “Is this all the planes to come back?” Tex nods. They all look so pale and wrecked. “Where's Red? Where's Skeeter? Hal?”

No one answers. They hang their heads and the exhaustion is palatable.

Corporal Hammon zooms up and halts the jeep and Colonel Jensen gets out. He gazes at the crew and looks worried. “Where's the Lieutenant?”

Tex points at Betsy. “Pulling himself together.”

Colonel Jensen hurries into the plane.

On the flight deck he sees the body on the floor and Red sagging over the column.

“Red,” he says cautiously. “Time to go.” He hears only a faint grunt. He walks across the now sticky, glutinous blood, and puts a hand on Red's shoulder. He speaks softly. “Come on, Red. I'll help you. I'll take you to the showers and get you cleaned up.” And he waits.

Slowly Red raises his head and looks at Jensen with dead eyes through a reddened mask of gore. The skin on his cheek in burned black. “Guess I'm a mess. Be a good thing to wash. Don't know if I can get up.”

Colonel Jensen slips his arm under Red's. “Lean on me.” He gets Red to stand on wobbly legs.

“You're going to get all stained.”

Jensen gets a tighter grip and turns him. "Not the first time."

Red sees Skeeter. His legs buckle. Jensen catches him and keeps him up.

A sob claws at Red's throat. "I'm sorry, Skeeter. I let you down."

"It's ok, Red. You did the best you could. You got the plane back." He pulls him away.

The crew stands around outside, too numb to move. Red drops out of the bomb bay doors and crumbles to his hand and knees. Jensen jumps down and helps him up, leading him to the jeep where a somber and quiet Corporal Hammon helps him into a seat.

Red looks at his reduced crew staring back at him. "You all head over to interrogation. I'll meet you at the tents." Jensen nods to Hammon and they drive off.

Corporal Hammon and Colonel Jensen wait in the jeep while Red stands under the "shower" - a water tank on stilts with a valve, which he opens and lets the water poor over his head and uniform. Desert sand sucks hungrily at the red water that pools under him. He turns it off and slogs to the jeep and gets back in.

Empty tents. A ghost town.

Survivors gather around Tex's small fire. Red opens his bottle of Tunisian brandy and takes a swig. He coughs as it burns like acid going down. He passes it to Tex who circulates it along with the other bottles floating hand to hand.

Red lies back and lets the blessed numbing wash over him. Arnie cranks up the old phonograph, now that its owner is dead, and plays the Fred Waring tune. "A Sleepy Lagoon" mourns with them.

There is no conversation. Silently they stare into the fire as they all sink deeper into the alcohol. Whenever the song ends, someone cranks it up again, over and over. The song croons, "a sleepy lagoon, a tropical moon, and two on an island."

Red takes another long pull on a bottle and looks over at Gus through the fog in his brain. The boy sits back from the others and hugs his knees. Tears cover his face in quiet sobs.

The next day Colonel Jensen sits at his fold-up desk, hands clasped in serious thought. There is a temporary look to the sparse office. His papers are in box files on two metal chairs.

Red sits across from him, the burn a large crusty scab across his hung-over face and hallowed eyes. "I keep thinking, if I'd started the evasive action sooner. If I'd dropped a foot or two, Skeeter and Hal would be alive."

"Stop it, Red." Colonel Jensen shakes his head. "Quit torturing yourself. You're lucky you got eight men back." He pauses then his voice hardens. "You can't whine about it when the killing starts."

Red locks eyes with him. "I guess you just never know when it's your turn, when the next canon shell has your name on it. That's how it works, doesn't it? You wait, we all wait and see if this is the mission we don't come back from." He can feel his voice rising and he pauses to breathe and consciously calm down. "You just never know what it's like until you're in the heat of it, with death everywhere and this time, just this time, it wasn't your turn." He stops himself again and sinks his head into his hands.

"That's war," Colonel Jensen says. "We've got to fight and not ask questions. And know that everyone of us is expendable if it means winning."

Red's head moves in a slight nod and his muffled voice comes out between his fingers. "That's what Tunisian brandy's good for, no questions asked. Us survivors get as numb as we can until our time is up and that fireball comes for us." His face comes up, looking vulnerable and haunted. "So I ask you now, how do we live after this war? What if we do survive? I forgot what it's like already to live like before, when blood and gore didn't stare me in the face."

Colonel Jensen sits back and doesn't comment at first. He regards a paper on his desk. "The 44th took a real beating this time. They're going to have to get us back to England to regroup with new men and planes."

"When do we leave?"

Jensen sighs. It's easier to deal with moving the squadrons around than the harder questions of surviving the war. "Maybe a week."

Red sits up. "I would like to ask you for a special favor."

"Anything."

"Let me and Arnie spend the next few days in Algiers. He met his family there." He pauses, "I met someone special too."

Colonel Jensen regards him with sympathy softening his eyes. "I don't see why not. Better than drowning in brandy around here." He reaches for paper to write the permission. "You can catch the supply plane. Leave me a number I can call to let you know when we're moving out."

Red rises slowly to his feet and salutes. "Thank you, sir."

Jensen smiles for the first time. "I want to meet this special person sometime."

"I'll make sure you do." Red starts to leave the room. Jensen stops him.

"One more thing. I put in for a promotion for you. Captain. Going to need you to lead, Red."

Red nods solemnly. "Thank you, sir."

He turns away and walks out the door, closing it quietly behind him, as excessive noise jars his aching head.

8

Yvette sits at her kitchenette table in a simple flowered dress, with her hair pulled into a ponytail, making her look like a school girl. She leans over a topographical map of France, phone receiver pressed to her ear, with a pad of paper on which she jots down notes. Something said on the other end of the line makes her grit her teeth angrily.

She responds in French, "We lost contact with them because you didn't come through with the supplies. They may all be dead by now! Damn you! How can you call yourselves French?"

She jumps at a knock on the door and quickly slams down the receiver, folds the map and pops open a hidden drawer on the table. There she stashes the papers and stands up. "Who is it?"

"Me."

She rushes to open the door. Red steps in with a lopsided grin and takes her in his arms. She pushes him away to look at the puckered scab marring his face. "Amour," she murmurs and lightly kisses the damage.

Then they are embracing fiercely, already pulling at the clothes that separate them from the desire of their flesh.

Late at night they lie on the bed, legs entwined. Yvette is draped in the Benghazi material Red had bought. He strokes her creamy skin from shoulder to thighs, over and over as if he can't get enough of the feel of her. As if her body and soul could wipe away the horrors he has experienced and take his mind to a warm, loving place where people no longer try to kill each other.

A candle flickers in the breeze wafting in from the balcony. Yvette stares into his face, memorizing the look of the man she has finally brought to her bed.

"One of us, or both of us could be dead soon," she whispers. He puts a finger to her lips, hushing her. But a tiny tear trickles from her eye. "Remember these moments. They are a gift from God to us in this terrible time."

"Always," he says, and kisses the tear away. She continues to stare into his eyes then turns her back to him and snuggles herself against him like a spoon.

"I have to go to London," she says. "The Free French are helpless here in Algiers. If our resistance fighters don't get help soon, all will be lost. I have to appeal to the Allies."

"Then we'll take you to England with us," he says with conviction. "We can be together, like I promised."

She cranes her head to look back at him. "Really? Can you make that happen?"

He kisses her softly. "Anything and more for you."

She wraps his arm tighter around her and closes her eyes. He feels the shudder of her breath. After a moment, he thinks she may have fallen asleep, but then he hears her voice speak in the quiet night.

"Cherish every moment, amour. This war will try us both."

He grips her body close, lost in the scent of her hair against his face, trying to block out images of sudden death.

Two days later, the apartment door bursts open and Red chases Yvette into the room and she laughs too hard to breathe. He catches her skirt and yanks her to him, nuzzles her neck and tickles her. She shoves him off and tries to catch her breath.

The telephone rings.

They both freeze. Their happy faces melt as if the very air were sucked out of them. Yvette picks up the receiver stiffly. "Oui," she says, listening. "Yes, of course." She hands it to Red.

"Yessir," he pauses. "I'll pick him up and we'll be back tonight." He looks at Yvette and crosses his fingers. "And Colonel,

I have a request to make. Yes, I promise this is the last request, at least for a while. Miss Yvette Leleu, Commander of the French Resistance needs transportation to England. She's on a mission to seek assistance from Allied forces and could really use our help. The French Resistance would consider it a great service if we helped her out, sir."

He listens intently and frowns then his face brightens. "Don, really? That's an excellent idea, sir. Thank you! Yes, tonight we'll be there." He hangs up the phone and scoops her in his arms, leaping onto the bed with her. She laughs and struggles.

"Well?" she squirms, dying to know the answer.

Red laughs, "Not only am I taking you to England, but I'm introducing you to my good buddy, Don Peterson, who happens to be liaison for Allied Headquarters. He will be delighted to meet you, I'm sure. And he may be just the man to help your cause. Besides, he owes me."

She hugs him, laughing with him. He rises to her lips and they kiss, softly at first, and then hungrily.

The squadron of B-24's drones loudly over Shipham Air Base as they circle above to land one at a time on the English tarmac. The day is overcast with steely gray clouds hovering over everything, rendering the environment equally colorless and cold. Shipham has the look of an old abandoned air base recently expanded to accommodate the American forces. Quonset huts look like tin cans cut in half and flopped over to fill the spaces around the ancient military cottages. No one bothered to cover the dirt with anything to absorb or repel water, so thick soupy mud coats the ground all around.

As they leave the planes parked off the runway, the crews slosh through mud as they jostle each other to find a spot to settle down and dump their duffel bags. Left alone without Red, his reduced crew moves among the huts to find one they can call home for now.

Steve pulls his fleecy flight jacket tighter. "Damn. We go from one extreme to the next."

Arnie tries to fake a British accent and fails terribly. "Bloody bad weather we're having. Must stay bundled up so as not to catch out death of a cold."

Tex looks tragically at the mud caked on his cowboy boots. "Gonna ruin my best boots! Never seen so much wet in one place in my entire life. We all gonna turn to rust and rot."

They move as a group toward the entrance to one of the Quonset huts, taking comfort among other fly boys in each other's company. They pick this one for its smaller crowd of milling men. They notice three men standing outside who are speaking quietly but urgently. Body language shows that two of them are confronting their pilot.

"Eddy, Pedro, you guys've got to leave me alone. I can't do this anymore. I just can't." The pilot seems to try to back away from his two crew members.

Eddy is a chubby, baby-face white boy who emphasizes his words with staccato hand gestures. "Look, boss, we've all been through it. Don't take it so hard. Let's just do our job and hope for the best. We've got to stick together now."

Pedro,a short and skinny Mexican with a face that's been in one too many barrio fights, steps up to his pilot and puts a hand on his shoulder. "We can make it. Come on, man. We need you, ese, blood brothers. Gotta keep going 'till we're done."

But the pilot continues to back away from them, shrugging off the comforting hand, panic widens his sleepless eyes. "No!" He wheels around and shoves his way into the barrack, slamming the door behind him. Red's crew stops in their tracks. They vacillate awkwardly there, wondering whether to try another hut or not.

Eddy turns to them looking deeply worried but trying to cover it up. "He just needs a minute. We'll give him a minute to cool off. He's having a rough time."

Pedro looks over the reduced number of the crew and asks, "Where's the rest of you?"

"Our pilot went straight to headquarters. We lost two over Austria," Tex answers. Pedro nods and there is instant camaraderie. By now in the war, all crews know what it feels like to loose members.

"We're all that's left of ours too," he says. "Our plane barely made it back. Pilot's having a hard time dealing with it all, you know, being in charge." He points at his partner. "This is Eddy."

They all shake hands like kinsmen. No one would ever understand lose like these men do now.

Sudden gun blast echoes from within the barrack. Eddy's face washes a sick pale and he yanks open the door. Pedro grabs at his partner as if to hold him back, or maybe to hold him up. His pilot lies in a pool of blood, service revolver fallen beside his gaping skull.

They all stand there in frozen shock. Every man in every barrack goes silent, knowing.

Red stands stiffly at attention in the 44th Headquarters at Shipham, while Colonel Jensen pins captain bars on his lapel. Jensen steps back, smiles and salutes. Red returns the salute.

"You look like a snake shedding its skin," Colonel Jensen comments, pointing at the peeling scab on his face.

Red touches it, wipes a few flakes off of the pink new skin beneath. "Thanks for the compliment, sir."

Jensen grabs his arm and leads him out the door. "Come. I want to show you something."

They slush out to the tarmac and off in the field where the planes are parked at their hardstands. Fabulously shiny new B-24's, fresh from the United States make an impressive row.

"New and improved," Jensen is saying. "They now have twin 50mm guns in the nose and a retractable belly turret. Increased fire power all around." They wander along and watch the young new crews in neat uniforms head toward the barracks in lost-puppy bewilderment.

"We've got a lot of work to do and no time to do it, Red,"

he says seriously. "I'm going to be counting on you and your boys to help train these new kids and get everyone up to speed. Missions are coming up. This war can't wait."

Red nods. They approach Betsy, sitting in the line like an embarrassing afterthought. The contrast of her multi-patched skin and motley scarred parts makes her seem ancient next to her sleek comrades.

"You can have any one of these new ships. We can give Betsy to one of the new crews. It's only fair."

Red pats her affectionately. "No. We fly her until she can't fly anymore. She's saved our asses more than once." He pauses, kisses her flank. "And she's bathed now in our blood."

Jensen nods solemnly. "And she saved Don Peterson's ass. Alright then, keep her. I'll make good on my promise and connect Commander Leleu with Peterson."

"I appreciate that, sir."

Colonel Jensen puts a hand on his shoulder earnestly. "Get these boys ready to face a mission in record time and I'll do whatever it takes for you."

Red grins, game for the challenge. "Yessir. Let's put crews together and fly this afternoon."

"Good man," Jensen grins and pats him hard.

Two candles are the only source of light in the small cottage. A bottle of fine wine and two glasses sit next to the candles, waiting. Yvette sits in the dark window seat, knees tucked up to her chin, her arms in a thick Cardigan sweater wrapped around her legs. She doesn't move and her dark hair cloaks her face so that no one would notice her sitting there if they entered and saw the lonely wine. She keeps herself tucked into a ball to combat the English cold that seems to seep into every inch of existence here. But her mind fights another kind of chill.

Red floats through her thoughts. She can't wait for him to arrive, and yet she dreads deep inside their budding relationship.

How can I even think to love another man? Not now, not in the throws of war. He will die. I will die. Fate will not let us be together.

But does she have the courage to cut it off, to disengage from this situation and fight the war on her own terms, only concerned with her own people? To get close to another human being requires risking her heart again. And how many times can it break before it kills her? From all she has been through, from seeing the invasion of her country and so much death, she can't shake the feeling that no one will survive this conflict. They are all caught up in a killing machine that wouldn't stop.

Hope, like a tiny flame, burns deep inside. That's why she waits for Red and allows herself the pleasure of anticipation. Against her will and her better judgment he has crept into her life and lit that flame, so delicate and so easily snuffed out, but it's there and glorious right now, for this moment.

The door opens and Yvette gets up from her dark spot and hurries into Red's arms. They kiss as if they have never kissed before, the need to feel each other so intense. Finally they sink into the chairs. Red releases her hands with a great sigh and reaches for the wine. He pours two glasses.

"My crew's complete now. Copilot Eddy Barber and engineer Pedro Gonzalez. We're going to set up squadrons tomorrow."

"It's all moving very quickly,"she murmurs.

He strokes her arms. She feels his warmth through the Cardigan. "I wish I could stop it," he murmurs.

She sits back, creating a space between them and swirls the wine in her glass , watching the blood-red liquid slosh. When she looks up, her eyes have hardened into a far-away look.

"My work moves on quickly also. There is no time to hesitate, and no time to think of anything but fighting. I will meet with your Don Peterson tomorrow in London. He seems willing to do anything to help someone who is connected with you. I believe you've made quite a friend." She pauses and her eyes bore into him with dark, smoldering emotion. "It is God's hand in our lives that connected you to Don and then to me. In this God-forsaken war, He still guides us to help each other."

"Yes," he nodded.

"If Don can get the supplies we need, I will go back to Paris very soon." She registers the anxiety forming in Red's eyes, but her look does not soften. "Our work, mon amour, cannot stop for us. I will have to go. Everyday I am away, my people are killed."

"You can't change that," he says with desperation shaking his voice. "You can only do what you can and pray it's enough."

"And what is enough?" she asks with passion behind her words. She takes a long swig of wine and plunks down her glass. "It is never enough while the enemy invades our country. Never enough to avenge the deaths of so many. No, my country needs everyone to fight."

They stare across the space between them, both with raw need in their eyes. Tonight they need to hold off all thoughts of war and give and take from each other.

Yvette moves from her chair to slide onto his lap. "Love me," she whispers. His glass spills in his desperation to put it down and scoop her up and carry her to the bed.

The entire newly formed squadron gathers in the hard-stand area to hear Red outline the drill. They are silent and attentive as he gestures and explains the procedure for flying formation. His own crew stands behind him, ready to move into action.

"That's it then," he says. "We climb and circle until we're all up and fall into our places. I'll be lead and watch from our tail. Let's keep it tight, boys, show 'em nothing but our guns. Move out."

Red and his crew turn to climb into Betsy. Some of the other crews point at her scarred body and shake their heads, snickering behind their hands.

In the sky over Scotland, Red sits in Steve's tail turret, radio to his mouth, and watches the novice crews line their planes up in squadrons. He talks to their green pilots.

"Come on, boys. Trust your speed and bring her in close."

Slowly they pull tighter and tighter until they create a formation with every angle covered by a gun.

He gives them the thumbs up.

In the afternoon, back in the briefing lodge, Red draws the formations on a black board in front of the seated crews. He marks some planes with x's to show them shot down then erases them and reshapes the squadrons.

"Be ready, be quick. Your ship's chances for survival and the overall chances of everyone else depends on you moving forward quickly and reforming. Our gunners need their best shot at covering our asses, so don't get caught up watching other planes blow up. Do your part and keep unity to your squadron."

Red looks over the little sea of faces. He tries to block out the thought that many of these men will soon be dead. He stands before them and grits his teeth against all emotion, portraying pure confidence. "Any questions?"

The men seem to relax a notch. Someone in the back raises a hand, one of the fresh recruits from the look of his snappy uniform. "Is it safe to tack on to your ship, Captain? Heard rumors your bird's got so much damage she could fall apart at any minute." Snickering quiets as Red rocks on his heels and grins at them.

"Let me tell you about my Betsy," he says. "She looks like a whore from the worst part of town, but she's dependable as hell. Seen my crew through the worst of the worst and been christened in our blood. Wouldn't trade her for all your flashy and fancy new ships if you paid me. You know what they say. The best lady is the one with experience."

They all laugh.

Yvette is dressed in a conservative dress suit of navy blue with a white blouse. No jewelry or any other adornments distract from her professional look. Her hair is slicked into a neat bun. She stands at a podium that bares the seal of Supreme Headquarters of the Allied Expeditionary Forces. Don stands beside her, quietly supportive as she addresses the Colonels and Generals from both the British and the American sides. The men stare at her with a mixture of fascination for her beauty and skepticism.

"I would like to conclude with a simple fact, gentlemen," she speaks her perfect English with the strength of her singing voice. "France is perhaps your greatest ally. Our resistance is far-reaching, capable, and organized. Help us and we can help you turn the tide of this war. Fail to supply us and we are doomed. You will have missed your greatest opportunity to strike back at our invaders. I trust that you will make the smartest decision that will benefit not only France, but all of our European countries. Every minute we take away from the Germans, every inroad we make is a victory that will save lives."

She nods to the assembly and steps away, letting Don lead her out of the conference room.

In the Shipham briefing lodge, crews assemble in the early morning cold, muffled in their thickest clothing against a bone-chilling fog.

Colonel Jensen is tracing yarn across a wall map from England to the Netherlands, down to Frankfurt, Germany. Their new mission is stark reality for all.

Night at Don Peterson's office in London and he taps nervously on his desk. He's watching Yvette load radio equipment into a large backpack. She is dressed completely in black, her hair disappeared under a black wool cap. She has smudged black on her face and the contrast between how she looked hours ago and now is startling.

"I don't see why we can't have our commandos do this," he said, not bothering to hide his frustration.

Yvette continues to pack the espionage gifts she has been given and doesn't look up. "Your men have no idea what it's like there. People get killed on all sides when you send in men who don't know what they're doing. I appreciate your concern, but as I told the Allied Counsel, all we ask for is equipment and back up. We are not asking anyone else to risk their lives for us."

Don's tapping becomes more insistent. "Really, you could wait a couple of days." He pauses, uncomfortable with what he wants to say. "Maybe you should at least take an extra day. Tell Red you're going. I don't want to be the one to tell him you left."

She turns on him, her dark eyes hard and gleaming through the smudged make-up. "I must go. Now. I have a job to do. If you don't want to tell Red, then don't. But I would appreciate it if you would, as his friend."

He sighs loudly, his fingers rapping loudly on the wood. "Damn it! I don't like this!"

She ignores his outburst and finishes closing the backpack. She heaves it on her back and it looks heavy. But she is already walking out of his office and he has to jump up and follow her out.

FRANCE – A single engine British Lysander floats just over the trees and settles quietly on the field. With no moon, the stars barely illuminate the sky and the uncultivated ground is as dark as black water.

One shadowy figure slips out of the plane, hunched under the weight of the backpack. She darts across the field to the far end where a farmer's truck waits in the trees. She jumps in and the truck starts up and drives away without lights.

In the morning light, high in the sky above the English Canal, B-24 squadrons fly in tight formation toward the Netherlands. P-47 fighter escorts buzz above them like guardian angels.

In Betsy's nose, Tex thumps his desk angrily. "Piece of crap."

Dominick glances up from his lookout position. "What?"

"This new radar system they equipped us with. They call it 'stinky' for a good reason. It's terrible and the Brits don't know what the hell they're doing."

"Just don't use it," Dominick suggests.

Tex groans with frustration. "I'm supposed to figure it out. Then I'm supposed to train everybody else on it. It's the Allies' new secret weapon to help us fly higher and do a hundred percent radar bombing with cloud cover. It's supposed to save planes, and lives too, though I doubt that's the biggest concern."

Dominick snorts. "Aren't you cynical today."

Tex peers into the radar again and shakes his head. "I can't make heads or tails of anything on it."

Dominick points out the nose window. "There's the Netherlands and the Luftwaffe's waiting for us. And there goes the Little Friends. They're leaving us." He waves at the P-47's as they head back to England. "What else do you need to know? Give it a rest."

From the flight deck Red watches Eddy's well-trained eyes rove over the gauges and handle the switches.

"How does she feel to you?"

Eddy flashes a quick smile. "Like a true lady-of-the-night who knows her business so well she purrs."

Pedro saunters onto the deck to check the fuel gauges and pats Betsy admiringly. "She's like my low-rider back home. Now that baby's sweet. Looks like shit on the outside, but wait 'till I paint her. She'll be queen of the barrio."

"Where's home?" Red asks.

Pedro slaps his chest with pride. "East LA, born and raised."

"Been anywhere else?"

The young man shrugs. "Flight school."

Red chuckles. "Well, you need to see the world. At least some of it."

"When I get back," Pedro says, his dark eyes glowing from his fight-scarred face. "I'm gonna travel all over LA. See Hollywood. Maybe see some stars riding around. Gonna fix up my low-rider and go cruising and people'll look at me with respect."

Eddy rolls his eyes at Red. "I keep telling him there's more to the world than LA."

Tex's voice resounds from the intercom. "Coast of the Netherlands."

Ed peers ahead. "Looks like they're waiting for us." Red too sees the Luftwaffe zero in.

Pedro hurries to the top turret ladder. "Let me at 'em!" He whoops like a bandit.

High over the Netherlands the air battle begins in explosive earnest. Wave after wave of ME-109's swoops down on the formation, trying to take out a bomber plane before they are blown out of the sky. They dive attack like little black birds pecking at bigger, slow-moving hawks. The Luftwaffe is relentless, swarming in, never giving up, bent on murmuring the big planes or committing suicide trying. Each bomber that is shot out burns and spirals down on fire or explodes like a small sun. The formation adjusts by tightening up quickly, never exposing a weak point.

Soon the sky is filled with colored and white parachutes and raining debris.

On and on they fly, all American pilots focused on getting to the target alive and every Luftwaffe trying to stop them. Now they make it over Frankfort, Germany, and Betsy, in the lead, opens her bomb bay doors. The other planes follow suit.

The German fighters back off as thick flak carpets the air in puffy explosions. A flak bomb bursts in front of Betsy's right wing and rocks her violently. Planes on either side move away to give her room to gyrate. When the smoke clears, number four engine is dead and eight feet of wing is sheered off. Struggling forward, she drops her bombs over the target and signals the others to do the same.

Another flak bomb explodes to her left and number two engine coughs and sputters with its propeller at half speed. The heavy plane loses speed quickly and drops out of the turning formation that leaves her behind.

On the flight deck, Red scrambles to stabilize the ship on two engines. Ed stays cool and watches the instruments.

"Mike!" Red shouts. He hears Mike answer from the waist.

"Gus is hit! Flak in his leg!"

Red grabs the radio and speaks. "Blue Leader to Deputy Blue, over. Tighten up that formation and take them home. We're hitting the deck. See you back at base and wish us luck."

Deputy Blue radios back. "Roger. Good luck."

Red and Eddy exchange looks, this is going to be tough. Red lets her sink down to skimming the trees and prays for invisibility. Both men sweat over the controls, trying to keep her stable.

They hear Pedro from the top turret. "There they all go." Like a lone goose that has dropped out of its V, they watch the formation fly away.

"Mike," Red calls, "How's Gus?"

Mike appears on the flight deck, wiping blood on a rag. "Stopped the bleeding, but a chunk of flak is still in his leg. Gave him a shot of morphine and he's sleeping like an addict." He looks out the windows at their damaged wings and watches Red struggling to guide her over the trees. "We gonna make it, boss?" In that moment he looks like the 18-year-old New Hampshire farm boy he is.

Red winks at him in a show of confidence. "Of course."

Tex calls on the intercom. "Crossing into the Netherlands. Change course 270 degrees."

"Roger," Red answers. "We're giving Pedro a guided tour so he can say he's seen more than LA." Pedro looks at him as if he is crazy. Here they are sputtering on two engines, alone in enemy-controlled territory. But then he begins to laugh. Only his pilot Red would find something fun about their predicament.

So all the crew members man the windows, watching the scenery pass quickly by, watching the rural countryside of the Netherlands with its pastures and villages.

A Dutch girl in wooden shoes pauses beside a windmill and looks up to see the deformed bomber fly over her head. She smiles and waves at Steve in the tail turret. He waves back enthusiastically.

Betsy zooms so low over the anti-aircraft gun embankment, the German soldiers have to duck. They race to their guns, but get there too late. Betsy wobbles out over the ocean.

Red has been trying to hold Betsy steady for hours now and his arms tremble with the effort. He looks ahead at the English coastline, searching for a tell-tale sign of relief. "Coming up on the base soon. Mike, radio that we need an ambulance for Gus."

"Roger," Mike answers from the waist.

Eddy flips the landing gear switches. They all hear the THUMP. "Only one wheel down. Know how to land on one, boss?"

"Of course," Red announces with automatic confidence he doesn't feel. "Mike, tell them we're coming in for a crash landing." He speaks into the intercom. "Tex, Dom, get out of the nose. Hang on everybody. This will be rough. Find something bolted down and hold on tight."

Betsy lowers herself like a wounded bird over Shipham runway. Her right wheel hangs like a broken leg. All engines die except for number one on the left wing. As her wheel touches down, her brakes burn rubber, her left wing is held high and then begins to lower.

She crosses the runway just as her left wing hits the ground and sinks into the mud and spins her in a loop to a stop. She lists there, dying, all engines silent now. Flopped on her belly, there is no way to get out but through the windows.

An ambulance zooms up and the medics pull Gus, drugged to semiconscious, out of the waist window.

Bob Garnes arrives in a jeep, jumps out and hurries to touch Betsy as if to feel her death throes. The crew crawls out of the waist window as the ambulance drives away. They all stand solemnly in the mud and stare at the irreparably beaten B-24.

Bob strokes her broken wing. "Poor girl. She was obsolete anyway, I guess. So this is it. She'll be scrapped now. I'm sorry we have to see her lying her in English mud all alone." He pets her mottled skin with deep affection. "Don't worry, baby. You're not alone. I'm here."

Red steps forward and puts his hand over his heart. "Betsy, you've taken care of us, and now you've brought us home again. Girl, you may look like a two-bit madam, but you're the best. We'll miss you and we love you." He hugs and kisses her body and turns to Bob. "And here's the man who kept her going for us. Come here, big daddy."

He moves toward Bob with open arms and his lips ready for the kiss. Bob gasps in horror and scrambles backwards, nearly falling in the muck. He stumbles to his jeep, yelling for the driver to step on it. They streak away.

Gus sits in bed in the infirmary, his thick bandaged leg rests on a pillow. His solitude weights heavily on him as he gazes out the night-blackened window. His head snaps around as he sees the crew file into the room. His face brightens.

"Hey there, Gus," Red greets him. "How's it feel?"

The boy blushes as they gather around him. "It hurts a little, not too bad."

Arnie bounces up and socks Gus in the arm, watching him grimace. "Amazing what some guys will do to get out of work. Now I'll have to cover for you."

"Now you're going to shoot both guns, one in each hand?" Gus asks.

Arnie turns to Steve. "Shrapnel must have loosened his tongue."

Red gets between them. "We heard they're shipping you back to the States."

A shadow crosses Gus' face. "Guess I go tomorrow. They don't let anybody hang out around here. Don't even give a guy a chance to get better." He looks down and swallows. It takes a moment for him to meet their eyes again and his are filled with tears. "Feels like I'm letting you guys down. I'm sorry."

"Listen, kid," Red puts a hand on his shoulder. "You've been one hell of a gunner and an important part of our crew. You got some metals coming too, for all you've done for us. You're part of our team and we won't ever forget it. Go home. Leave this war behind. You deserve it." He adds softly, "We'll miss you."

Each man takes a moment to shake Gus' hand. Tex whispers something that makes the boy smile. Arnie looks like he'll cry and he leaves quickly. The others follow.

Gus stops Red. "I want to thank you. Tell you how much I respect and admire you. If I could be different that what I am, I'd want to be like you. I was lucky to be on your crew, and I saw how you really looked out for us. So thanks, Captain Crazy Red. Sir."

Red doesn't speak, his head down, trying to control his feelings. He holds Gus' hand. "So long, my good friend."

Gus' tears begin to trickle down his face. "See ya Stateside."

Red nods, walks away and shuts the door. Gus slide down in the bed and pulls the sheet over his head.

9

In a dank, dark root cellar in Paris, an old fashioned kerosene lamp puts out a dull illumination with its wick turned down low. Claude leans over his compact radio and listens. He is a small Frenchman with a big hate for Germans. Yvette stands over him and waits. They are both dressed in black with their heads covered in wool caps and their faces soot-blackened. It is hard to tell them apart, without seeing any hair and with Claude's short and slight build. But his body belies an aggressive strength he would gladly use against the invaders.

He says in French, “The plane dropped the supplies. They're coming in.” He turns and looks at her and his dark eyes show the respect he feels, glowing from his smudged face. “Your plan works so far.” Hope has sparked a new light and warmth to the chilly room. Yvette ventures a fleeing smile.

He nods, “Let's hope your Americans are consistent.” He packs the radio in a backpack and she dons another. Both strap on weapons belts with revolvers and knives.

“Maybe you'll learn to trust,” she says.

He stops and grabs her arm, a sudden burning look in his eyes. “Trust no one, mon cheri. And stay alive.” She pulls free, blows out the lamp to complete darkness.

Outside of Paris a German blockade is heavily guarded with soldiers and lights to ward off the black night. Troop transport trucks line the side of the road with a convoy of sleeping soldiers ready to roll into Paris in the morning. The blockade is wooden and with strung barbed wire and a detail of guards. More guards pace back and forth along the road.

One guard walks up the hill from the trucks and meets another and, after sharing a cigarette, he relieves his comrade of duty. Alone now, he watches the trucks below. No one sees him, so what the hell, he lights another cigarette. A guy needs something to do on a cold, boring night.

A black shadow slips up behind him. Yvette's catlike figure makes no sound at, nor does the black knife in her hand reflect any light. Fast as a panther, she grabs the guard's helmet, yanking his head back and slits his throat. His rifle falls quietly as she pushes him down to gurgle at her feet.

Six black shadows join her and they move soundlessly down to the trucks. There they plant explosives as they move. Then they are gone, melting into the night.

A quiet moment prevails.

BOOM, boom, boom! A chain reaction of explosives picks up the trucks, the troops, the ammunition and tosses them into the air in obliterating fire. Screams don't have a chance to echo over the deafening sound.

Red and his crew admire the sleek, brand new B-17 sitting in the hardstand. Bob rubs her shiny skin with his rag, looking like he wants to kiss her. "She's a beauty, ain't she?"

The crew whistles appreciatively. Whitie and Lowel crawl out of her bomb bay doors and grin.

"Everybody wants to fly a B-17. She's like a Sunday drive in the park," Whitie says. They all notice that he's wearing nothing but a T-shirt and coveralls tied at the waist. Lowel looks stuffed in his fleece coat under zipped coveralls.

Red nods to the perpetually dreary overcast skies. "This weather agrees with you, eh, Whitie?"

Whitie tilts his face up, extending his arms luxuriously. "A white man's dream."

"I never been so cold in all my life," Lowel grumbles miserably.

Whitie slaps Lowel's padded chest with admiration glowing in his eyes. "Don't listen to him complain. The local girls are eating him up. He gets a few new ones every time we go to town. They love his black ass." Lowel grins and turns away.

Corporal Hammon skids his jeep to a stop and Colonel Jensen jumps out. Another man hops out and bounds after him like a hyper puppy. He is a short five foot two and squirrely with rolled up cuffs where his flight suit is too long and baggy for him. His young eager face looks like a school boy signing up for a soccer team.

"Red, boys, I want you to meet your new waist gunner, Bill Fieti," Colonel Jensen says.

Bill nods to them all, too wound up to stand still, he shifts back and forth on his feet. He waves and grins with a silly twist to his fresh mouth. "Hi y'all. Just call me Billy. Or you can call me Ferret. That's what my pa calls me. Said I was good at crawlin' around under houses fixin' pipes on his plumbin' jobs." The Southern drawl and grinning deliverance makes them all smile.

"You'll fit in perfect," Red says. "This is the craziest crew in the fleet. We got a reputation to maintain." Bill bounces on his feet, chuckles and sort of snorts.

Arnie looks skeptical. "Can you shoot?"

"He means more than crap down the pipes," Jacob adds sarcastically.

"Hell, yeah!" Bill looks like he's going to leap up and down. "Let me at 'em! I can shoot anything that moves. My first toy was a pistol and I could shoot coon by the time I was four." He rubs his hands together enthusiastically. "Show me them Germans and I'll shoot 'em up! Can't wait to get at 'em!" Arnie and Jacob take a half step back away from his wild gestures.

Colonel Jensen steps in and pulls little boxes out of his flight jacket pockets. "Something else just came in. Your promotions. Can't have this crew leading without rank."

He smiles as he pins Captain bars on Tex, Dominick's and Eddy's lapels. He turns to Red and his smile widens. "Major Red Rider." They salute each other as Red gulps down his sudden feelings, deeply humbled.

"This is fast, sir."

Colonel Jensen puts a hand on his shoulder. "One thing about war is there's no time to think about it. When good men rise to the surface, you've got to take advantage. You're one of the best."

True to his name, Red blushes and bows his head.

The Colonel turns to Tex. "How's it going with the new radar? Winter's coming and the Allies are counting on us to figure out how to use it."

Tex pulls a rolled up aerial photo from his flight suit and moves over to a barrel to flatten it out. They all move with him to look, giving Jensen room to stand next to him. Bill bounces from foot to foot in the periphery.

Tex points and explains. "Couldn't figure the scope out, sir. So I had them take photos over Scotland for mock-up targets. I compared the photo to what I saw on the radar and I can start to see the target. We went up once and tried it and it worked. If I can get some more of these photos, I can train the other navigators to read it too."

"Excellent," Colonel Jensen pats his back. "I have faith in you. Anything you need, just ask. I'll make sure you get it."

Tex rolls up the photo again. "I'll take a couple of navigators up with me this afternoon and see if I can train them. Should work."

"I'll call Headquarters with the news," Jensen shakes his hand ecstatically. "You boys can lead the first Pathfinder radar bombing missions." He turns and pounds Red's back. "Rather historic, isn't it, Major? Your crazy crew is making history right here and now, and Pathfinder missions are going to change the tide of the war. The Germans won't have a chance. Good work, all of you. Carry on."

The Colonel steps back to his jeep, ignores the stream of tobacco spit Corporal Hammon lets fly, and hops in.

At the guest house Red lights the two candles and looks around the room slowly. Solitude. Everywhere he can see her, feel her, but she isn't there. He picks up her black dress lying on the chair and smells it and stares at her hair brush under the mirror.

He moves to the phone and dials.

Don Peterson sits alone in his office, concentrating on the papers he is reading and signing.

The phone rings.

He reaches for it. "Yes? Go ahead. Hey, Red! I figured you'd call. Of course I'm still here. No rest for the weary." He stops smiling and sits up, getting serious. "She's ok. And she knows what she's doing. You've got to trust her." He shakes his head. "Listen, SHEAF Headquarters is happy with her progress and they're backing their word with more supplies. Her people have been transmitting information on the Germans nonstop. They're our eyes and ears over there."

He leans back in his chair, stacks his feet on the desk and speaks more softly. "I don't know, Red. You've got to let her go and do her job. It's what she wants to do, what gives her purpose. And she's damn good at it. I wish we had dozens like her with that kind of passion and dedication. I'm sorry this war has to draw in a talented lady like her, but it is and there's nothing else we can do." He sighs heavily. "Yes, I'll call you. Get some rest. Good night."

He hangs up and clasps his hands together, a worried frown over his face.

Red sinks slowly to the bed and grabs a pillow that bears her scent and lies down, clutching it.

In the Normandy Province the mist and silence lie heavily over the farm land. Clomp, clomp of the old mare's hooves echoes on the road. She pulls an ancient, worn out buggy. An old man dressed in worn out pants and coat, scarf around his face under his old hat, prods her and clicks his tongue. A haggard woman slumps in the seat beside him. She too looks like a poor peasant woman, bent over with age and a hard life. They roll over the rise and suddenly see the village.

Something is wrong.

Mist smells of smoke. A blanket of it sits over the houses.

Through their disguises Yvette and Claude exchange a glance.

Outside the village, Claude halts the mare and points. A hastily dug pit stretches along the road with abandoned shovels strewn around it. Yvette jumps out and runs to the edge of the pit, forgetting to look old. She gasps with a hand over her shawl-covered mouth.

The pit is filled with bodies of village men and boys, bullet wounds making blackened and bloody holes in their coats. Some of the boys look as young as five, their bodies tossed in among the chaos of limbs and heads like an afterthought. The Germans didn't bother to cover up their deed, but left them like swept-up garbage.

Yvette spins around and gets back in the buggy. Claude sees the stone-hard look in her eyes through her old-woman face. He slaps the mare onward.

The street's cobblestones are chewed up from tank treads. Doors to empty houses hang open. With the misty smoke sending tendrils through buildings and the eery silence, they could be locked in some nightmare where all humanity is erased and nothing is left but the vestiges of their village.

Claude and Yvette ride into the plaza. Where the church once stood is now a smoldering mound of ashes. They hop out of the wagon and walk up the soot-covered stone steps that now lead to nothing and gaze over the smoky ruins. The heat hits them in a cruel wave.

Yvette stares at the ash mounds and begins to discern a piece of a necklace here, a skull there, a hip bone protruding, and suddenly blackened bones take shape over the whole floor.

"They locked them in here," she gasps, backing up. "Locked them in and burned it down around them." Her voice catches and a strangled sob emanates from her throat. The hands that clutch at her shawl are shaking.

"We must go," Claude says and attempts to pull her, but she has planted herself on the edge of the step, staring back with her old-woman face illuminated by the glowing heat.

"Just wiped out an entire village," she barely utters.

Claude pulls harder and she lashes out at him, slapping his hand off her arm. Anger consumes her and she storms by him and climbs on the buggy. He settles next to her and clucks at the mare to move, glancing at her from the side.

Like a volcano, her eyes erupt in tears that threaten her makeup. Claude concentrates on the road, unable to comfort her, his own fury already burning out his heart.

Steve watches the incredible sight from his ring-side seat in the tail turret of the B-17. The 8th Air Force lines up in squadrons behind them. B-24's and B-17's spiral up out of the clouds to form a flying parade of power.

Steve leans into the intercom. "When this war's over, we're never going to see this again. And nobody's going to believe it if we tell them."

P-47's and RAF Spitfires lace patterns of white condensation above them.

Red's voice comes over the com. "Twelve thousand feet. Go on oxygen. Heading for green flare at 26,500 feet."

Steve flips his mask on and continues to watch the Allied armada lift higher above the cloud-shrouded world where all is white and blue and brilliant. For a fleeting second he thinks about God. He must be looking down on these unstoppable legions going into battle for goodness and freedom. A powerful feeling swells Steve's chest and tingles through his body.

"If I die today, Lord," he murmurs softly, "It will be for something special and I know You're with us."

In the waist positions, Arnie looks at Bill who does a little dance around his gun.

"What's the matter with you, man?"

Bill grins at him, all energy, like a kid on too much sugar. "Where are the turkeys? Time for shootin'!"

"Calm down," Arnie gestures at him. "You scare me."

"Too bad we can't get close enough for a trophy," Bill checks his gun for the thousand time, and peers around out the window. "If we was on the ground, I'd be pulling a helmet or somethin' off a dead Hun. My girlfriend sure would like a trophy. She likes me to bring her somethin' every time I go a huntin'."

"Girlfriend?" Arnie looks skeptical. "She must like 'em small. Hell, you're shorter than me!"

Bill grins at him like a madman. "Small? Not where it count. Try this on!" His hand rubs down the inside of his flight-suited leg and outlines a very long, semi-engorge, dangerous-looking penis. Bill laughs at Arnie's shocked gasp.

"Man alive! You can have a free-bee at my whorehouse any day. Bet my girls would appreciate it. Satisfaction guaranteed!"

Bill nods magnanimously. "Thanks." He turns back to his gun and window and starts to whistle while gyrating like a nut.

In the sky over the North Sea, Red's ship shoots off the green flare and the armada levels off at 26,500 feet. Almost immediately German ME-109's zoom in and the P-47's and Spitfires lock them in a dog fight battle, trying to keep them away from the lumbering bombers. Desperately the Luftwaffe try to break through, but the Allies fight like tigers. Little planes blow up all over the sky, dropping parachutes, bodies and debris on both sides.

One German fighter manages to slip through and dives at Red's lead plane, but meets a wall of solid lead and explodes.

Bill jumps up and down at his smoking gun. "That's right! Bye, bye baby!"

In the nose, Tex studies the "Stinky" radar, comparing it with his photo of the target. He stares out the window and down, ignoring the raging battle above their ship. All he can see is white cloud cover as if the world did not exist. His eyes rove over each of his sources of information, from the radar to the pictures to the white nothingness again, then he calls on intercom to Dominick who waits in the bomb bay.

"Ready, Dom?"

"Ready."

He focuses another moment, not breathing, trying for precision. "Ok, bombs away."

"Bombs away!"

They all feel the opening doors, the massive weight of bombs as they drop out and create a sudden lift for the plane.

The entire armada follows Red's lead ship and bombs pour out of them to fall en mass through the clouds. At the same time, great puffs of flak burst among them, peppering the ships.

Two planes take direct hits of flak and are torn to shreds and rain all over the sky. The armada turns back to the North Sea as a fresh wave of P-47's flies in to back off the Luftwaffe.

On the flight deck, Red gazes out the window at the white-blanketed world.

"We must have hit something." The insecurity emanates from his subdued voice.

"Have to have faith," Eddy says, hoping beyond hope that he is right.

Red grabs the intercom. "Tex, did we hit the submarine pens?"

Tex's voice booms back at them, sounding comfortingly sure. "By my calculations we did. Besides, you can't go wrong with that many bombs. We carpeted the place! But hey, if we missed it, I'll be sending you my suicide note."

"Eddy's just reminding me to have faith. So that means you too, cowboy."

"Yessir!"

They head roaring back to England.

The next morning, Red and the crew hang around the plane at the hardstand, watching Bob, Whitie and Lowel check the engines. The steady drone of planes is a constant noise as new crews pour onto the base.

Bob, at the top of the ladder, holds on to a propeller and points to the cloudy sky. "Something big's a brewin'. This place wasn't built for this many crews, but more are coming every day."

Whitie pokes his head out of the engine. He is grease streaked like a zebra in his minimal t-shirt and pants. The white of his skin shines brilliantly through the black smudges. "I heard they're amassing all kinds of soldiers and boats all over the coast. Heard it from the girls in town. They're being more selective now they've got more men to choose from."

Tex dashes toward them through the mud in his ruined cowboy boots, waving his arms. "We did it! It worked!"

He produces a paper and, out of breath, reads it. "Strike photos of Emden, Germany's submarine pens, show direct hits! The target's been destroyed!" He looks up, beaming a huge smile as the others cheer.

"Cause for celebration,"Arnie says. "Let's cut out early and head for town."

"It's eight o'clock in the morning!" Eddy exclaims. "Want to get us all court marshaled?"

Arnie pouts at him. "Just wanted to warm up the ladies before the town's flooded with guys. Hate competition."

Jacob steps over to Lowel's ladder possessively. "I'm hanging around Lowel. That gets me attention."

Pedro postures himself like a Zootsuiter, strutting around the group. "I get attention all by myself. These English chicas like brown boys too."

Tex waves his paper at them in frustration. "And the point to all that was, we clobbered our target and used the radar. Good news, and all you guys think about is your dicks." He turns away and heads back to base. "I have more important things to think about, like training navigators. See you all later."

They watch him go and shrug it off. Eddy pokes Red. "What do you say, Major? Shall we hit the town tonight?"

Dominick stands behind Red and gestures frantically at Ed to stop. Red looks from Eddy's puzzled expression to Dominick who scratches himself and whistles innocently.

"We understand if you can't come with us, boss," Dominick stutters. "It's ok."

Red gazes around the group as they stare at him. He smiles and shakes his head. They look relieved. "You boys have fun. I'll be busy tonight." He leaves them and climbs into the ship.

Bob comes down the ladder and gathers them close, whispering and shaking a finger at them, "There's a lesson in that, my boys, you'd better not forget. It's fine to hit the town and look for some action with the girls, but don't give your heart away while we're fighting a war. Anyway you look at it, means pain. Your boss is in a world of hurt right now."

The crew glances at each other, nodding.

Somewhere in the Normandy Provence the moonlight sifts coldly through the forest. A group of men and women dressed in black materialize in a small clearing. They all kneel as if in prayer around Yvette and Claude and a cluster of backpacks. Claude takes a compact transistor radio out of a pack and demonstrates its use. Yvette hands a backpack to each group leader. No one speaks. Solemn blackened faces study Claude's gestures carefully.

Yvette suddenly stands, a hand up, listening. Everyone freezes. She brings her hand down as if cutting the air with a sword and they grab their packs and fan out in different directions. They melt into the trees and are gone.

Seconds later, shots ring out, tearing up the silence. Men shout and dogs bark savagely and the clearing fills with German Shepherds and soldiers. They spin around for a moment, not sure which direction to turn, obviously frustrated.

Red hangs up the phone, sitting in the dark of the cottage with only a hint of moonlight coming in through the window. He doesn't want any light. It might shine through the bravado he has been masquerading all day and show his true fears.

And crush him.

Don can tell him nothing new, and that may be worse than getting bad news – not knowing anything at all. Don said that she is doing dangerous work and can make contact only on her terms. The intelligence she is providing has proven to be invaluable to the Allies, as well as a great boost to the Resistance fighters, but he said she is in more danger from French traitors than from the German's. Of course, nothing he said can alleviate Red's anxiety.

So here he sits, in the dark, his head sinking into his hands. For the first time all day he can let the waves of pain wash over him and feel it, for Yvette, for Skeeter, for Hal, for his old friend Denny and the family he left behind, and for all the comrades who have died so far in this crazy, senseless war. Never has he felt more vulnerable, knowing that there is nothing he can do but keep fighting.

But tonight there is no fight left in him. He shuffles to the bed and throws himself on it, and perhaps he even cries.

The streets of Shipham are bustling. Groups of American and British soldiers, sailors and fly boys fill the sidewalks. Local girls chatter at the men with flushed cheeks and flirtatious eyes. They wear their dresses tight and skirts flippy on this cold English night.

Tex leads the crew as they pick their way through the crowds, maneuvering around the drunks and the couples who make-out lustfully. Jacob, Arnie and Steve surround Lowel like body guards. They wave and smile at the women who stop to admire the black man's complexion. Whitie brings up the rear, wearing his minimal t-shirt and pants, fresh washed, and swinging his arms out expansively.

"Come and get me, ladies. Yes, that black guy's my brother. You have to go through me to date him."

They pass a dark, recessive doorway and see a woman with her back pressed against the door, having sex with a soldier who holds her leg up. Her dress conveniently covers the act of their joining.

Mike jumps away, startled by the sight. Dominick grabs him and pulls him along down the sidewalk.

"What the hell are they doing?" Mike asks, horrified.

Tex calls back from the front of the group. "They call it the English-doorway-quickie. For some, it takes care of business."

Dominick slaps Mike's back with a grin. "Some of these

girls are professionals and they offer the service for the horny and the desperate, for a fee."

"Well, I ain't payin' for nothing," Pedro says, strutting along like a Mexican cock. "I'm gonnna get mine free. Orale!"

Bill bounces around the periphery of the group, looking at everything at once. "Damn! I forgot my license."

"For what?" Mike asks.

Bill grabs the outline of his very impressive crotch. "For my weapon."

Arnie jostles Mike whose eyes widen at the sight. "Don't ask him to explain or show you any more."

They pass other doorways and alleys where the same service is in practice. Mike grimaces at the sound of grunts and squeals.

"I'm gonna find a sweet little gal and teach her the Texas slide," Tex comments. "I'll show her there's more to us Americans than a quickie."

Dominick points to the open door of a busy and loud pub. "And that's were we'll find our sweet gals, I'm sure. Let's go!"

They all pile inside.

Inside the pub, men cluster around the tables and along the bar in separate groups – Army, Navy, Air Force. The beer flows from great kegs and slops in mugs that aggressive, fast-moving waitresses distribute. Smoke hangs in a haze over their heads.

The crew shares a crowded table with another group of airmen after Eddy and Pedro introduced them. The copilot, happily drunk, sits next to Eddy with his arm over his shoulders. "So how's it going, Eddy-boy?" he slurs.

The engineer leans into Pedro and pokes him jovially. "We heard you guys are with the famous Crazy Red."

"Yeah," Copilot says with obvious admiration despite his lubricated state. "The one who picked up hitchhikers at Ploesti and caught a German sub."

"Now you boys are in the lamb light," the engineer adds.

The navigator glances at Tex with respect written on his

face. He's not nearly as drunk as the others. "Lead Pathfinders. You guys should go down in history. It's an honor."

Tex smiles humbly.

"For sure your crew will lead at D-day, whenever it happens," Copilot says, sobering to the conversation.

"They can't keep it a secret," Eddy says. "Not with all these men and equipment. More arrive everyday."

Navigator nods. "They say the only thing keeping England afloat are the barrage balloons."

Arnie snort, "Bet the Germans are shitting their pants."

"No." Jacob says, his voice hard with hate. "They're the superior race, remember? They think they can still win." The passion of his hatred causes several of the men to slide mugs of beer in his direction. He is definitely not drunk enough.

"All I'm hoping," Tex says, adjusting his Stetson, "Is that the big boys figure out how they're going to do it and do it right. Not like Ploesti. That was a disaster. You'd think they'd have more information and make better plans." He sighs, exasperated. A sudden and heavy silence has fallen over the men. They are all remembering air battles and death and what if feels like to march into the thick of it, not knowing if the next flak bomb or cannon shell has their name on it. For a moment no one moves, all eyes down cast. Then they look at each other and feel, on a deep level, that they are among brothers in a way only they can know. They all nod, hold up their mugs and toast. As the glasses clink, they know they are also drinking for those who never came back.

A group of giggling English girls enters the pub. Steve stands up quickly. "Time to show the girls my love handle."

The others stumble after him to vie for attention like peacocks.

10

D-DAY JUNE 6, 1944

Two hundred B-17's spiral up into the stratosphere. They emerge from the predawn darkness of ground, up into the sun beams that stretch from the curve of the earth to light the celestial world.

They gather like a flock of geese and sail out over the water at 20,000 feet. The panorama of planes fills the air as the ocean far below boils with thousands of ships heading for France.

Tex studies his radar unit in the nose of the ship. Dominick paces around in the small space, wringing his hands.

"It took too long to get us all in the air," he says anxiously. "We're already delayed. If we bomb when we get there we could be bombing our own men. I can't do this."

Tex glances up at his buddy, tilts his hat back. "We're ok. Relax. Just a little delayed. Maybe the ground assault's delayed too."

Dominick turns on him with an intensity Tex has never seen in the quiet Virginian. "Don't you see how it's all shot from the start? They only gave us a 15 minute leeway! You heard them at the briefing. We have to bomb right on time or risk bombing our own troops." He whips around and puts his hands on the window, leaning on them. "They should have picked somebody else for this. I can't be the one who blows up Americans and British soldiers. They should have planned it better. Watch, you'll see, it'll be just like Ploesti, only a bigger disaster for the ground soldiers. Can't do it. Just can't."

"Stop it, Dom," Tex frowns at him. "You're lead bombardier 'cause you're with me and I won't steer you wrong. Get a grip on yourself. You have to do this."

Tex stands and moves toward his friend's back, tries to put a reassuring hand on him. But Dominick shrugs him off, his eyes glassy with fear.

"Look, Dom, we have to bomb that embankment or the Germans will mow our boys down as soon as they hit the beach. That's our job, soften up the resistance. If we don't succeed more will die." Tex moves back to his radar screen. "Get in there, Dom. We're coming up on the coast. I'll give you coordinates."

Dominick hesitates then disappears into the bomb bay.

Red glances out the window of the flight deck through scattered clouds and sees the Normandy coastline full of landing barges with thousands of soldiers struggling through the waves to get to the beach.

He speaks into the intercom. "Tex, are you ready? Dom, ok?"

Tex calls back, "Comin' up on Omaha beachhead. Ready count down to bombs away."

Dominick's shrill voice cracks over the intercom. "Look at the time! We're late! Two hundred planes behind us are going to bomb our troops!"

"Get a hold of yourself!" Red says. "We're ok!"

"On our bomb run now," Tex calls. "Open the bomb bay doors. Feed your bomb sight with these coordinates. Count down. Five, four, three, two, one. Bombs away!"

Utter silence.

The armada zooms over the bluffs above the beach, over the German cement bunkers.

Red and Eddy exchange a look of utter dread. They hear Tex scream, "Bombs away, damn it!"

The plane suddenly lightens as she spills her load. They hear Tex continue to shout. "You overshot the target! The bombs are falling behind the fortifications!"

Silence.

Red leans into the intercom. "Back off, Tex. What's done

is done. We're heading back to base to reload. Let's worry about this afternoon's mission." He pauses, closing his eyes. "Dom did what he thought was right."

They turn back over the sea and leave the ground battle behind.

They fly away from the high western sun, straight into Northern France. Red is looking around out of the window and grumbling to himself.

"What's that?" Eddy asks, more to quiet his pilot than to find out what he is saying.

"This is crazy."

"What is?"

Red shakes his head. "We must have hit our target on the beach head. Must have. Otherwise they would have sent us back to bomb again, or maybe not. Damn, I don't know." His voice trails off again. The entire crew feels the weight of worry. On the biggest assault and the most important day of the war, could they have missed the target?

"We must've hit it," Eddy says.

"Yeah, well, now they want us to fly all over France and bomb whatever we see that the German's could use. Seems kind of..."

"Disorganized?" Eddy points at several other six-plane B-17 groups, just like theirs, flying low over the French countryside. They all crisscross and look like lost children. One group drops bombs on the railroad.

Red peers down at an abandoned village below them. "Sure hope the squadrons are careful where they bomb. Civilians have been through enough already."

"This is just chaos." Eddy agrees. "I thought the big leaders would have fleshed out a tighter plan. Strange directive to just come here and bomb anything we see." Eddy glances at Red, and risks probing. "You worried about Yvette?"

"Always."

Red points to a railroad bridge ahead. "We'll hit that." On

the intercom he says, "Bomb bay open, Dom. Coming up on a target."

Pedro's voice calls frantically. "Look up, man! They're gonna kill us!"

Red and Eddy lean forward and look up into the open bomb bay of a B-17 over their heads. They watch in open mouth horror as the bombs roll out and drop on their group. Miraculously they fall right through the formation and straddle Red's wings.

"Holy Mother of God!" And Red peels off in another direction, leading his group out of the way. He wipes the sweat off his face. "Did I say this is crazy? You can't send a bunch of bomb-packed planes to fly around looking for anything and everything to hit. Some idiot is going to drop 'em and run."

They come up on a highway bridge. Red looks around first then gives the order. "Let's blow this baby. Go ahead, Dom."

Their bombs hit it full force. The bridge shatters like glass.

"Ok, enough of this madness," Red announces into the intercom. "Tex, give me a heading that'll take us over Omaha Beach on our way back."

He tries to sound casual, but he can feel the tension on the ship. They all want to see what happened on the biggest day of the war when they had played such an important role. Did they play their part well? Had they backed the Germans off of their positions on the cliffs above the beach? If not, what happened to the thousands of soldiers landing there?

The answer comes too quickly.

Their group flies high through the clear sky as the sun dips for a crash landing in the sea. They swoop down over the bluffs above Omaha Beach.

The cement bunkers of the German gunners look intact.

Dominick jumps up from his seat and presses himself against the nose window. "No,no,no," he cries.

Below them lies a carpet of bodies over the sand. Some float in the water, caught in barbwire obstacles, while soft waves lap red over the bloody sand. Blown up landing barges list, half-submerged at odd angles. Not a stretch of beach can be seen under the mess and tangle of dead men.

Dominick slides to the floor. "Oh my God! What have I gone?" Before Tex can get to him, he has crumpled into a sobbing heap.

An ambulance meets Red's plane as they roll to a stop off the runway.

Red rushes into the nose to find Tex on the floor holding Dominick who has his flight jacket pulled over his head. Tex coos and rocks him.

"It's all right. I'll take care of you," the cowboy murmurs into the jacket.

Red stoops to help lift Dominick. Tex turns his gaze on him with desperate eyes.

"He'll be alright, won't he, boss?" he asks. "Everything'll be alright."

"We'll take care of him now, Tex." Red tries to assure him as he guides them out to the ambulance attendants.

Red stands on the tarmac and with his crew gathered around him as the ambulance takes off. "It wasn't his fault," he mumbles. Each man is weighted down under silence, bone-weary and numbed by the horrors he has witnessed today. Those who have experienced the emptiness of camp after a battle of too many losses will remember this night as one of the most silent and deadly.

Then they move as one down the path toward the debriefing building as evening descends with the ever-present chilling fog.

Tex steps out of their barracks as the rest of the crew approaches. They stand under the light outside the door and look expectantly at Tex. Full night and tendrils of fog give the place an eery quality. This is not the place of bustling energy it was just last night. The few sounds heard are distorted and distant, as if only the ghosts of all those who died this day have come back to bunk in their abandoned barracks.

Only this crew stands here, alive and waiting to hear word of their friend.

"The doctor tried to give him a shot, but he refused," Tex says, nodding to the door. "He's in there now on his bed."

"Think he'll be ok?" Eddy asks.

Tex shrugs, looking tortured and exhausted. "Wish I knew. He won't say anything to the doctor. Hell, he won't even talk to me. Hasn't said a word since -" He lets it drop. The scene of Omaha Beach is already too sharply imprinted on all of their minds.

They stand there awkwardly for another moment, wondering if they should go in and try to talk to him or simply drop on their own bunks and sleep the exhausted sleep of the dead.

Tex shuffles there, staring down at his ruined boots. "Can't help him if he won't talk to me. I tried to get him to see, there was nothing else we could do. Just following orders. Nobody blames him."

Red puts a hand on his shoulder. "It's ok. You're doing the best you can do. Should we go in and -"

"Did you take his pistol away?" Eddy asks with sudden urgency.

Tex's face goes pale and he whips around to grab the door.

A gun blasts from inside the barracks. The crews' eyes pop wide. Tex dashes in as Red reaches for him and charges after him, screaming, "No, Tex! Don't go in there!" Arnie, Jacob, Steve, Mike and Bill hurry to try and stop them.

Only Pedro and Eddy stand stock still, unmoving, their faces ashen as their minds relive this same scene, still so fresh. Tremors shake their bodies.

The crew, Red, and Colonel Jensen stand at attention in their pressed uniforms and watch as a casket is loaded onto a cargo plane. When it disappears inside, the crew turns instinctively to Red. Colonel Jensen shakes his hand, pulls him close to speak in his ear, and walks away.

Red gazes over his men. “At this point, we'll either wait for a new bombardier or they'll split us up into other crews.” He sees the distress in their eyes and it overwhelms him. He has been a father figure to these boys, and right now he feels spent and useless, unable to protect them, let alone hang on to them.

“You guys are the best crew ever,” he chokes on the emotion. “I'll try to keep us together, if I have any say at all in this business. Now I want you to take the rest of today off. Go into town. Rest for a couple of hours.”

They hesitate, staring back at him like abandoned boys. Red is suddenly struck by deja vu. Has it been less than a year since they stood staring at him as fresh, young recruits on the Benghazi desert? How many horrible scenes have they experienced together since then? How much tragedy have they witnessed? Some of the faces are gone now, replaced by others. But they are brothers in blood and he hopes like hell he can keep them together.

“Go on. Get out of here,” he says softly. As a group they turn and trudge away, walking close, side by side.

Only Tex stays behind. “I just need to know,” he says, fighting for control of his tears. “Was I friend enough for Dom? Did he know how much I cared about him?”

Red takes hold of his shoulders and gazes hard into his eyes. “You were the best friend a man could ever ask for.”

Tex drops his head and lets the tears slide down his face. He nods and backs away. Red lets him go. For a moment he wonders, as he has so many times before, how they will get over what this war has done to them.

Corporal Hammon zooms up in his jeep. He has to spit to speak. “Major, they want you at Colonel Jensen's office. Phone call from SHEAF.”

Red leaps in beside him and they take off.

Red rushes into Colonel Jensen's office. Jensen sits at his desk, holding the phone. “Ok, put him through.” He hands the phone across the desk. Red takes it, noting the emotionless face of his superior officer.

"Rider here. Don, what's going on?" He listens intently, sinking slowly into a chair. Jensen turns away from the look that washes over Red's face.

"I'm going in there. Tonight. You contact him. Set it up. I'll radio you for the details from the air." He hangs up hard. Colonel Jensen keeps his back to him, gazing out the window.

"I can't sanction you taking a B-17," he says to the window. "But I don't always know what's going on at night around here."

"Thank you, sir."

"Twelve hours. That's all you've got."

Red hurries out the door.

Red is strapped with a service revolver and a rifle as he steps into the dark hardstand. He stops, surprised. The crew, including Bob, Whitie and Lowel are waiting for him.

"We heard," Bob says quietly. "Thought maybe you could use a hand."

Red pauses, choked up, looking at their shining eyes in the black cover of night. "I can't let you guys risk it."

Tex steps forward. "We're not letting you take on the whole German army by yourself. No argument. We're going."

Red shakes his head with a grin. "Crazy bunch of nuts."

Bob pushes a box toward them. "You might want to take these along for the hell of it." He pops the top and exposes a case of grenades. He pats the plane. "She checks out and she's ready to go. The tower's going out for coffee in," he consults his watch with a flashlight, "Fifteen minutes. All's clear."

"How'd you?" Red starts then stops. He chuckles. "Damn, your resources stretch far and wide, don't they?" He slaps Bob hard on the back. "I owe you, my man."

Arnie and Steve grab the grenade box and haul it into the plane and the rest of the crew follows quickly, before Red can say any more.

Whitie grabs his crotch. "Gassed her up myself. A hundred proof."

Red throws an arm around his neck and squeezes. "What would I do without your body fluids?" Lowel pulls Whitie away.

Bob taps Red's shoulder. "She's even got a special feature we just installed. Should be useful for your field landings." He turns his flashlight on the wings revealing two sets of rockets. Bob beams at him as if his big face were going to split. "Jato pods. You push a button and they jettison the ship on independent canisters. Great for when she needs that extra push before she hits the trees." He continues to smile gleefully at Red's shocked face.

"You were supposed to try it out and see if it works under controlled conditions, but I guess tonight's a good time to start."

Red is humbled and his face shows it. "How did you know? How did you do all this. For me."

"Told you a long time ago. Nothing happens around here without me finding out. Got my sources and I'll never tell. You ain't the only one who loves me around here, I'll have you know. Besides, you didn't think you could have flown away without help, did you?"

"But the grenades? The tower's coffee break?"

Bob grins secretively. "Which reminds me, you better hurry up." He gives Red a shove. "If anybody can pull this off, it's you, Crazy Red. Just bring my fly baby back."

Red gives him a quick bear hug before he can react, and bounds into the plane.

In the Normandy Province, the B-17 skims the trees then drops to the ground as a fallow field opens below her. She bumps and rolls to the other end, turns and stops. Engines cut out.

The crew emerges, hangs in the shadows of the trees, each equipped with a rifle and grenade belt.

Long moments pass and they hear the putter of a tired engine. A milk delivery van comes down the dirt road with its lights off. It stops and a man hops out and runs across the field. He halts before Red and proffers a firm hand shake. He has the look of a guerrilla warrior with a lean, muscled body and hard, assessing dark eyes, the kind of man who is comfortable in dangerous places, who lives for the challenge.

"I am Philippe," he says with a thick French accent. "You risk much, mon ami."

Red shrugs. "Yeah, well, don't we all."

Philippe cocks his head. "But you do not need to do this thing. It is our fight here."

"No," Red says, staring down at the smaller man. "It's all of our fight."

Philippe nods to this, gestures toward the van. "We must hurry."

They start to follow him when Bill clatters loudly out of the B-17, lugging his waist gun.

"What the hell?" Red says.

Arnie hurries to help him carry it. "How'd you get that off its pod?"

Bill grins triumphantly, the ammunition belt slung over his shoulder. "My pa's plumbing taught me everything I need to know."

Philippe shakes his head, muttering something about crazy Americans. They head for the van.

Red and the crew sit on the floor, crammed together with the waist gun lying across them. Philippe speaks in French to the driver who watches the unlit country road with eagle eyes. He too is dressed like a peasant, with a cap pulled low over his forehead.

Philippe turns to Red. "We intercepted message from Germans on radio. They say they have Resistance fighters trapped. They calling for tank and more men."

Red nods. "Where?"

"Close to here."

"And the tank? When will it get to them?"

Philippe frowns. "It comes now. We have not much time." He stares hard at Red as if he could see right through to his heart. "Maybe she is dead."

"Maybe she's alive."

Philippe suddenly smiles and nods.

Sniper fire rings through the trees. Philippe leads them to an open spot on the wooded hill from where they get a view of the bombed out village below. A radio man hunches over his transmitter behind a log. He is dressed completely in black with soot-smudged face and wool cap. He speaks in quiet French to Philippe and points to a long, sleek Gestapo car and a troop truck parked down below, at the edge of the village. German soldiers crouch behind ruined walls and shoot at a brick building that still stands, though windowless and fire-blackened.

Philippe scuttles over to Red and whispers vehemently. "Our group caught the traitor." He mutters a long string of French curses. "Such a man does not deserve to exist."

Rifle fire from the brick building makes the Germans duck.

"Who knows how much things he tells to Gestapo. He died a traitor." Philippe puts a finger to his head like a gun. The radio man whispers to him again.

"Tank is very close. We go now or no time."

At the outskirts of the village, Red, Philippe and the crew fan out and creep down the hillside. The Germans have their backs to them. A Gestapo officer in a crisp uniform and cape paces back and forth beside the safety of his car. He glances at his watch with impatience.

In a sudden volley of shots, the officer is slammed back against the car with a look of utter surprise. The Germans along the wall crumple over the bricks. Two Germans hop out of the truck and are cut down.

Philippe leads the way over the wall. He shouts in French as they dash down the street to the brick building. Red stops, sees a body wearing a backpack lying in dried, thickened blood.

The backpack is riddled with machine gun bullets. Philippe rolls the body over. Claude looks up at them. He is almost gone. Philippe tenderly touches his bloodless face.

Claude's voice rasps. "I have been waiting for you."

"We are here now," Philippe answers. "You see, I bring Americans."

Claude's eyes glaze with a painless, celestial smile. "Good Americans. Go. Get her out of this. Enough. Enough."

Air seeps out of him with the last of his blood.

Philippe stands, a hardened warrior with tears in his eyes. Red glances at him, knowing exactly how he feels to lose one more friend to this damn war.

"He's gone," Red says. Philippe nods. The crew hangs back and watches. They are grounded fly boys out of their element. They haven't seen the war from this level before and no one can figure which is worse, an aerial battle or this guerrilla fighting. Both seem to have the same results, comrades who die in front of their eyes.

"Come. He must not be killed for nothing," Philippe says, and they follow him into the building.

They step into the total darkness of a rubble-strewn floor from the collapsing ceiling and walls. Philippe calls. A voice answers from the front room.

They hurry in and see two men crouch by the gaping windows with rifles and empty boxes of munitions spread around them. They slump against the wall, exhausted and taking advantage of this reprieve. Philippe kneels by them and speaks quietly. One murmurs and points to another room.

Red doesn't wait. Heart pounding, he rushes into the room.

Yvette lies amid the rubble, looking lifeless and pale. Red falls to his knees beside her and checks for a pulse.

"She's alive," he calls to his crew who stand in the doorway. He sees bloody rags that were hastily stuffed in her black shirt against a shoulder wound. With no one to apply pressure, her blood has leaked from her.

Philippe drops next to him and roughly rips open her shirt to expose the wound. A bullet has gone through the muscle from the front and splintered her shoulder blade in the back. She is unconscious, cold and unresponsive.

"We've got to get her out of here," Red urges.

Philippe rips the rags up smaller and stuffs them into both holes then pressurizes them with his belt. "She will die. She won't make it anywhere."

"We've got to move now," he starts to pick her up.

"Crazy American, you cannot hope for too much."

"Yeah, well, that's what they all call me anyway. Let's go." Red stand, cradling her small body in his arms. They all start to turn to the door and freeze.

Rumble and screech of tank tread echos through the deadly quiet.

An explosion disintegrates the brick wall and knocks everyone to the floor. Sound evaporates as their ear drums ring.

The crew scrambles to their feet and Tex grabs Red, helping him gather up Yvette and make a dash for the exit. The two soldiers in the front room lie dead under an avalanche of bricks. Philippe pulls his leg out from under the rubble and follows them, limping.

They struggle up the hill, Tex pulling on Red to help him climb. The crew shoots back at the Germans who flood the village streets, following their tank. Arnie and Steve hold Philippe between them and shoot with their free hands. They still have several yards to go to get over the hill, but now the German bullets begin to sing around them. Jacob, Bill and Mike pull grenade pins and fling them hard. Explosions turn German shouts to screams. The tank cannon cranks as it turns to line up with the hill.

The crew sprints wildly, sweeping Red with Yvette and Philippe along.

BOOM! A tidal wave of dirt flies everywhere, obscuring the night. And then Tex is charging through the smoke and earth, pulling Red and leading the crew over the top. Behind them the Germans start up the hill and the crew lobs five grenades at them that blow up the first line and bodies are catapulted in the air.

The crew bursts through the trees and heads for the van. The French radio man and the driver wave at them frantically. Red gasps for air, with Yvette flopping like a rag doll in his arms. They reach the van and the Frenchmen help them climb in. Arnie and Steve toss Philippe at them and turn to face the German troops as they make it over the hill and rain bullets down toward the van.

The tired old engine won't turn over and the driver grinds the starter in desperate panic. Pedro shoves him out of the way and hot wires the engine in an instant.

"Jump in!" he shouts as he burns rubber on the gravel road. He grins like a crazy bandit at the dazed Frenchman. "Just like back home in LA!"

Bill sits at the open back door of the van and lays his 50mm cannon from the plane across his lap. As the van bounces along, Bill holds tight and blasts at the Germans, cutting them down as they emerge from the trees. They are thrown backwards and torn to shreds.

"Yeeeehaw! Feathers flyin' now!" he screams over the racket. Jacob, Steve and Arnie toss more grenades that blow up in a wall of dirt and fire. They cling to whatever they can hold on to as Pedro careens along the road.

Red wraps his arms and legs around Yvette's still body, trying to buffer and warm her. He doesn't dare check her pulse or look at her injury. Fear of losing her is overwhelming him. But he can feel the sticky wet of blood seeping between them. All he can do is pray.

Philippe groans in pain. Tex pulls up his pant leg and loosens his boot to expose the man's ankle swollen twice its size and purple. Philippe grabs Tex's hand. "Thank you."

"What for?"

"You should have left me there. We almost not make it. Thank you save me."

"Oh hell, we're all in this together, right? All of our fight?" Tex grips his hand and grins.

They hear the buzz of motorcycles and trucks approaching as they jump out of the van and dash for the B-17. Bill lugs the waist gun with him. Red carries Yvette.

Philippe waves from the back of the van. "Take good care of our princess."

"I will," Red nods gratefully. They scramble aboard as the van speeds away and motorcycles zip down the road. Red lays Yvette on the flight deck and wraps her in his flight jacket. Eddy starts the generator and one by one the engines whir in sync.

Steve scurries into the tail turret, slips in his seat and rotates his gun on the approaching motorcade. He shoots and they flip in the air like popcorn.

Red joins Eddy at the controls.

"It'll be a miracle if the Luftwaffe doesn't find us," Eddy says.

"Just keep praying for more miracles. Mike!" Red yells. Mike rushes on deck.

"Lie down with her and wrap yourself around her. Try to keep her warm."

"What?" Mike asks in shock.

"Do it!" Red shrieks. Mike jumps down and engulfs her little body in his. He blinks up at Red.

"You sure about this, boss?"

"Just don't move."

The plane vibrates with the sound of waist, tail and top turret guns blasting. Eddy points at the newly-installed Jato button.

"Do we dare?" he asks.

"Hell, why not."

They taxi on the field and push her over the rough ground. At 60mph Red pushes the button. He and Eddy are slammed back in their seats. Mike, holding Yvette, shoots across to the back of the deck.

Four jets come alive under the wings and boost the B-17 off the ground and over the trees.

11

Yvette moans in the hospital bed. Her pale face is flushed feverish. A thick bandage wraps around her entire shoulder and extends down her arm to immobilize it. A hospital gown covers the rest of her.

Red reaches a hand to stroke her matted, sweaty hair. Tex and the rest of the crew stand close, surrounding her bed. They move aside as Colonel Jensen and Don Peterson squeeze through. Whitie and Lowel peer over the others' shoulders, trying to get a glimpse of her.

Colonel Jensen leans toward Red. "How's she doing?"

Red shrugs, his eyes never leaving her. "Doctor said she should be ok. This fever is burning her up though."

"We're going to transport her out of here, get her Stateside as soon as possible," Don says, placing an assuring hand on Red's back. "I promise you, she'll get the best care possible."

Yvette's lips move as if in conversation and her head rolls slowly side to side. They all hold their breath and watch with worried frowns.

The head nurse bustles into the room. She's a Scottish matron with an impeccable white uniform stretched over a well-padded and muscular frame. She glares at the men as if they were enemy intruders in her ward.

"You'll all be backing up a bit, I tell ya. Let that poor girl breathe." Hands on her hips and murder in her eyes, she makes them all step back. Her gaze only softens when she sees Red gripping Yvette's good hand and stroking her forehead.

Whitie sidles up to the nurse and grins. "We're just watching over her, ma'am."

She huffs at him but moves away. "Another ten minutes and ye all get out of here." She closes the door as she leaves.

Yvette's eyes flutter open. She focuses and sees Red holding her hand. The others move up closer. Her voice is rough and barely audible. "Am I in heaven?"

Steve pipes up, "Yup, and we're your angels, sweet heart." The others elbow him in the ribs.

Yvette shifts her shoulder and pain lances through her eyes. She closes them to suppress a groan. "We were trapped, Claude and I." Her eyes fly open and she grasps Red's hand. "Is he dead?"

Red nods and she turns her face away as tears track down her cheeks. "I thought we were both going to die. I was shot first and then he fell on me to protect me." She takes a ragged breath. "I thought you'd never know where or how I died. I'm so sorry."

Red kisses her hand and wipes her face. "You're safe now."

Don steps closer and she nods to him. He smiles. "I'm afraid you and I are both victims of Red's hitch hiking habit. You were all lucky to get out of there."

She settles back on the pillow and they can see the pain etching across her face, exhausting her. Don frown down at her. "But I'll tell you right now, you're not going back. You're going to have to let Philippe and the others handle things. And that's an order."

"I second that," Red says, kissing her cheek.

She closes her eyes again wearily. "When my people are free, it will be over. Not until then." But she is fading away and Don and Jensen corral the boys out of there to leave Red alone, holding her hand.

1952

A sleek, black limousine slides up to the stage exit. Fans back up and wave at the tinted windows. They stare at the exit with anxious anticipation.

A body guard, dressed in a fine suit, opens the door and scans the crowd with unblinking military eyes. He opens the limo.

Yvette steps out of the theater, looking spectacular in a long, glimmering black gown. She pulls a scarf of Benghazi silk out of her bag and drapes it around her neck. The fans cheer for her and she dazes them with a brilliant smile. She steps up to the limo and peers at the window

The door opens and a hand extends toward her. She smiles and takes it, slipping inside.

Driver opens his window and it's Pedro who leans out and cocks his cap at the body guard. "Another beautiful night in Hollywood, eh amigo?" Pedro winks and settles back in his driver seat. The window rolls up and he maneuvers the limo slowly through the fans. They shout and wave as it pulls away. The license plate reads: CRAZY RD.

The limo glides down the boulevard and passes under the marquee of a movie theater. Bold letters proclaim: RED RIDER STARS IN PATHFINDER.

A lawyer sits stiffly in his office chair, looking somber in his gray Italian suit and graying hair. He peers at papers on his impressive mahogany desk then looks up to regard Janet Wilson as she nervously twists her purse straps, sitting across from him. She wears a modest dress of a working widow and the strain of these years without Denny has left worry wrinkles around her eyes and mouth.

"I have asked you to come here today," the lawyer begins solemnly, "to inform you that your mortgage has been paid in full. The children have substantial trust funds that should pay for all of their educational needs."

He gazes across the desk at her, adjusting his glasses over a poker face. She frowns at him as her mouth drops open and she begins to sputter. "But, I don't understand? How can that be? The Air Force wouldn't have paid anymore." She turns pale with fear. "Where did the money come from? Who do I owe?"

Before she can work herself up to tears, the lawyer sits back and presses his hands together. "Madame, please. There is no mystery here, no debt to pay. Let me say that your late husband had a good friend who presently wishes to remain anonymous. He wants you to know, however, that he made a promise to Denny Wilson which he intends to keep. Please accept this token of his friendship."

He watches her face crumble into tears of joy and offers her a box of tissues.

A stewardess attends to four businessmen as they sit at a table in the plush seats of their private jet. They have the air of important decision makers as they quietly discuss the papers on the table.

One man whispers to the stewardess who nods and knocks on the pilot's door. She opens it and Eddy turns to her, looking sharp in his crisp uniform and bright smile.

Brooklyn, New York, Arnie bounds out of his house then turns and waves. His wife, a pretty dark-haired woman from Algiers, steps out the door with a baby on her hip and waves back at him.

He strides down the street, greeting neighbors as he goes. He turns the corner into the business district of town. Shops line the street. Shopkeepers open up, sweeping storefronts and changing signs to OPEN.

Arnie approaches a large hardware store with shiny tools of all kinds displayed in the windows. The sign says: ARNIE'S HARD W-HOUSE.

In a radio studio, Mike watches for the signal with headphones on. A green light flashes on.

"Good morning, Manchester," he says brightly in his New Hampshire accent. "Mike here on the mic." He chuckles. "Isn't it great to wake up in this lovely state. Ehya, love New Hampshire!"

In the morning, like clockwork, the doors open of two houses in the modest, middle American neighborhood. Two young boys of mixed race exit their respective houses and move together at the sidewalk. They join the stream of children heading for school.

Whitie exits his house as Lowel steps out of his. They also meet on the sidewalk and turn back to wave at their wives who come out to say good-bye. Whitie's wife looks like Lowel's sister and Lowel's wife is a sweet blond.

Tex rides his horse to a knoll overlooking the long stretch of Texan range, dotted with cattle as far as the eye can see. He stops, contemplating the vast, silent country.

The drone of a jet breaks through the cloudless silence as it streaks across the sky.

Tex watches it go and smiles.

Made in United States
North Haven, CT
04 May 2025